Fateful Affairs

A story of murder, mystery, and love

PETER EISENHUT

Fateful Affairs

Copyright© 2022 By Peter S. Eisenhut.

All rights reserved. No part of this book may be used or reproduced by any means, graphic, electronic, or mechanical, including photocopying, recording, taping or by any information storage retrieval system zwithout the written permission of the author except in the case of brief quotations embodied in critical articles and reviews.

This is a work of fiction. All of the characters, names, incidents, organizations, and dialogue in this novel are either the products of the author's imagination or are used fictitiously.

Bennett books may be ordered through booksellers or by contacting:

Bennett Media and Marketing
1603 Capitol Ave., Suite 310 A233
Cheyenne, WY 82001
www.thebennettmediaandmarketing.com
Phone: 1-307-202-9292

Because of the dynamic nature of the Internet, any web addresses or links contained in this book may have changed since publication and may no longer be valid. The views expressed in this work are solely those of the author and do not necessarily reflect the views of the publisher, and the publisher hereby disclaims any responsibility for them.

Any people depicted in stock imagery provided by Shutterstock are models, and such images are being used for illustrative purposes only.

Certain stock imagery © Shutterstock

ISBN: 978-1-957114-55-2 (Paperback)
ISBN: 978-1-957114-56-9 (eBook)

Printed in the United States of America

Also, by Peter Eisenhut

The Pen Project
(Saigon 1967)
Copyright 2016

Boulder Creek Project
(Colorado 1987-1988)
Copyright 2018

Final Project
Copyright 2021

I dedicate this story to Brandy.
She deserved better.
May she rest in peace.

-1-

BRANDY'S NIGHT OUT

He sat in his rental car in the parking lot outside a popular bar and lounge in Albuquerque, New Mexico. It was a warm Friday evening, the 24th of July, 2015. He had spent the week doing reconnaissance and hoped that tonight it would all pay off. He was Latino with tan skin, black hair, average build, and no unique features. Others hardly noticed him. After all, half the population in Albuquerque was Latino. He wore brown slacks and a tan short-sleeved shirt—nothing out of the ordinary. Visually, he was just your average Joe. But his mission was nothing but.

Inside the lounge, Brandy enjoyed celebrating the end of a busy week with her colleagues from the nearby Sandia Labs. Brandy was a middle-aged woman with a successful career. Her colleagues liked and respected her. Tonight, she had no need to hurry home. Her only child lived in California, and her husband had told her he would be in Santa Fe until tomorrow.

He patiently waited for Brandy to exit the lounge and return to her car. Earlier in the day, he had magnetically attached an explosive device to her Audi A-4. He strategically placed it near the engine, high up behind the right wheel well. It only took about 60 seconds and he didn't think anyone saw him do it. Finally, after more than two hours she returned. He didn't mind the wait. The more she had to drink, the easier his job would be. The time was now eight-thirty, the sun had already set, and it was getting dark. From his perspective, the darkness would make it even better. He watched her get into her car and start the ignition. The explosive would not detonate until he depressed the button on his remote activator. That would happen later.

She was alone and would be on her way home. He was totally familiar with the highways and avenues around the city and knew where she lived. He followed her for about a mile until they were on a stretch of road most appropriate for the event. They were on a divided highway with two lanes in either direction. At this time of day, traffic was light. Brandy was in the left lane and had just passed another vehicle. He depressed the button on his remote activator, braked quickly and pulled off the highway to the left. The explosion damaged the Audi's right front axle and steering rod. It also blew out the tire. The sudden damage caused Brandy to lose control. Her Audi slowly spun clockwise and crossed in front of the vehicle she had just passed. Then that vehicle clipped the rear fender of Brandy's car as it tried to avoid a collision by veering to the left. That vehicle stopped further down the roadway on the shoulder of the left lane. Steam poured out of its radiator. Meanwhile, Brandy's Audi traveled sideways and backwards and finally came to rest on the right shoulder of the roadway.

Everything was proceeding as planned, he thought, but his mission was not yet complete. He quickly turned on his emergency flashers, exited his car, and ran across the road to Brandy's Audi. She was beginning to stir, but flames were starting to appear all around the passenger side of her car. As intended, the explosion ruptured the fuel line that entered the engine compartment near the right wheel well. As he approached, he could see that she was already trying to undo her safety belt and leave the car. He couldn't allow that to happen. He opened the driver's door. He had to act fast.

"Where do you hurt?" he asked.

She was semi-conscious and moaning from pain, but seemed to understand.

"All over," she responded, slurring her speech.

Perhaps it was whiplash, perhaps liquor, he thought. However, he did not think her injuries were life threatening and she was about to get herself out of the car. So, he took the next step.

"Let me help you get out. Your car is on fire and may explode," he told her.

As they talked, he retrieved a small case from his pocket, opened it, and removed a preloaded hypodermic needle and syringe. As his left arm reached across her body as if to release the safety belt, his right hand jabbed the needle into her arm. It only took a few moments for the drug to take effect. She went limp and he returned the used hypodermic to his pocket. He was about to head back to his car when bright lights exposed him. Another car had pulled up and stopped behind him about 25 yards up the roadway. He had no choice. He removed Brandy from the car and carried her limp body up the roadway toward the bright lights and set her down. A man got out of the stopped car and approached him.

"What happened?" the man asked. "Can I help?"

"Yes, please call 911 for me. This lady's car is engulfed in flames. It could blow up at any moment. I pulled her out, but she's unconscious and needs an ambulance. Meanwhile, I need to move my car. It's over there partially blocking the left lane. And there's another car involved in the accident. It stopped further down the road on the left. I need to see if he's okay."

The man acknowledged and called 911 on his cell phone.

Meanwhile, the "Good Samaritan" went back to his car, climbed in, and drove off. With the darkness, he doubted that anyone would have read his license plate.

-2-

THE TRIP

Five and a half months later, Joey Francisco Ramirez was on his way back to his home in Albuquerque. He had spent the last two weeks visiting his stepson in San Bernadino, California for the Christmas and New Year's holiday. Joey and his wife Brandy had made this trip together each year since their marriage three and a half years ago. But not this year. Brandy had died in a car accident almost six months ago. His stepson had insisted that he not cancel the trip, and he was glad he didn't. The year 2015 had been bittersweet for Joey. His visit had given him hope that 2016 would be better.

Driving alone on a long stretch of interstate highway can be boring without another form of mental stimulation. On the way out, Joey had played Christmas songs until he was sick of hearing them. On the way back he had tried music and the news, but today he wasn't in the mood for music and he didn't think the news was worth listening to. His visit with his stepson had been joyous and cathartic. He had played with Brian and Lucy's six-month-old son and they had opened presents and laughed together. It was a happy time. But now he was suddenly alone again and feeling depressed. It was as if he had just fallen off a cliff. A part of his mind continued to drive the car, while another part of his mind began to reflect on the circumstances surrounding Brandy's death.

Just before her death, Brandy had purchased a new car. Her new car was a Lexus RX 350 Sport with all-wheel drive, the same one he was driving now. The car was a pleasure to drive on a long trip. Joey enjoyed the car's many features—satellite radio, superior sound system, heated and cooled front seats. You name it. Unfortunately, Brandy never got to drive it. The car had not yet arrived at the dealership when Joey had to leave on a business trip to Santa Fe. So, Joey had one of his employees do the driving to Santa Fe, and he had left his Audi A-4 at home for Brandy to use while he was away. She was driving his Audi when she lost control, collided with another car and went off the road. When the New Mexico State Police notified him, he was devastated. He loved her.

Investigators couldn't find a cause for the accident and had ruled her death suspicious. Brandy was a good driver. Her blood alcohol level was below the legal limit, and she didn't use drugs. Her injuries did not seem consistent with her death. Her death was suspicious and an investigation ensued. Two witnesses described a person of interest who looked very much like Joey. The police thought Joey may have had something to do with her death, but he had an alibi. He was in Santa Fe on business when the accident occurred.

He remembered the funeral service and the interment of Brandy's ashes. Everyone was there—all their friends, people from their respective employers, family members, and Ed. Ed had come all the way from Costa Rica. He was a friend of both him and Brandy and had been a friend of Brandy's mom, long before that. Ed had also been a business associate. If it hadn't been for Ed, he never would have met Brandy. After the funeral, Joey and Ed discussed the circumstances of her death. Ed said he would support Joey in every way possible.

The investigation had stalled. The investigators needed more information. After her death, Joey had received a message that mysteriously showed up on his computer screen.

My love and my career.
Now your turn. See how it feels.

The sender did not identify themselves. However, the message led Joey to believe that Brandy's death may have resulted from a past relationship. He didn't know if it was a personal relationship or a business relationship. Ed had already advised him to be careful what he shared with the local police. He had past relationships that he couldn't afford to reveal so he never told the local police about the message. The message had reminded him that he bore some responsibility for Brandy's death. The feeling of guilt was hard to shake. He had tried therapy and it helped, but despite so called doctor patient privilege, there was a limit to what he thought he could safely divulge.

As he headed east on Interstate 40, daylight faded and the skies became overcast. Traffic was slowing. He stopped reflecting on his past and turned his full focus back to the road. He turned on the weather station and heard them forecast heavy snow in the Flagstaff area. As he got closer, the weather worsened. Snow began to impair his vision and accumulate on the roadways. As in the past, the trip home from San Bernadino would take two days with an overnight in Flagstaff, Arizona. He already had a prepaid reservation at a hotel where he and Brandy had stayed the previous year. He expected to arrive late afternoon. He was glad he had a hotel reservation. He could not have driven much further—not in this weather.

He checked in to the hotel around five-thirty and went up to his room on the second floor. It was a premium room with two queen-size beds and all the amenities you could ask for. He stared at the beds for a moment. He would miss sharing one of them with Brandy, but he put the thought out of his mind and headed back down to the lobby.

Right now, he was hungry. He looked out the doorway—looking bad he thought. No need to risk driving in this mess. The hotel had a bar and a restaurant. He would eat here.

-3-

PICK UP

He walked through the lobby and made his way to the Skyway Bar and Grill. As he did so he was aware of an air of excitement, something unnoticed only twenty minutes earlier when he checked in. There seemed to be more people and more voices. He reached the entranceway to the bar and grill and was about to enter when a hostess appeared, ushered him back, and planted a signpost in front of him. "Please wait here until a seat is available," she said. Joey looked past the entranceway. To the left, a crowd of people—mostly men—had gathered around the bar. To the right, people sat at the tables in the restaurant. He saw none that were available. Within moments, others began to line up behind him.

He turned to the person immediately behind him. She was a young woman of medium height and build with dark brown hair tied in a ponytail. She wore jeans, a flannel shirt, and fashionable boots. He found her facial features to be appealing with no apparent makeup. Her light tan complexion gave her a healthy outdoor look. Strung over her shoulder, she had what appeared to be a large saddle bag. To Joey, she looked like she had just ridden in on horseback. Eager for friendly chitchat, he initiated a conversation.

"You know this place is really buzzing. Seems like a bus load of people just arrived. You have any idea what's going on?"

"Sure do. You nailed it. A bus load of us just arrived. They closed the airport and cancelled our flights. They took us to different hotels for food and overnights."

"Wow, sounds like you're stranded. Will you be able to get another flight tomorrow?"

"Don't know. Right now, things don't look so good for tomorrow. They're predicting the worst snowstorm in ten years."

"May I ask where you're headed?"

"Albuquerque."

"Interesting. That's where I'm headed as well. I live in the northeast sector of Albuquerque. How about you?"

"I don't live there yet. My aunt lives there. I'm from Cornville."

"Where's that?"

She chuckled. "Few people have heard of it. It's a small village, south of Sedona and just east of Cottonwood."

"Is it far from here?"

"About an hour when the weather is good. In case you're wondering, by the time they canceled my flight, the roads were too bad to risk having my friend come back to get me. I didn't want her stranded here as well. She was already back home when I called her and we talked about the situation. But . . . I don't understand something. You didn't seem to know about the airport closure."

In his mind he gave her credit for her keen observation. "Well, that's because I'm *driving* to Albuquerque. I was in California visiting my stepson for the holidays and I'm—"

Just then, the hostess appeared and said his table was ready.

"Listen, would you consider sharing a table with me. We can talk about Albuquerque and it will save you a few minutes of wait time."

"Okay," she responded. "I'm eager to learn about Albuquerque."

The hostess led them to a small table for two, and handed them menus. The young woman removed the bag from her shoulder and set it next to her chair, and Joey removed his sport jacket and hung it over the back of his chair. As soon as they were seated, Joey spoke.

"I should introduce myself. I'm Joseph Ramirez. Friends call me Joey. And before you ask what I do, here's my business card." He handed her one of the cards he kept handy in his shirt pocket.

"Hmm . . . *Business Security Systems*," she read off his card.

"And what about you?" he asked after she hadn't offered.

"I'm sorry. I'm Debra Johnston. I'm not currently employed, but I just got a nursing degree and I hope to get licensed in New Mexico and start a new life."

"What was wrong with your old life?" he asked half-jokingly.

"A lot. My father died about four months ago. I found his body. I could tell he was poisoned, but I had to convince the first responders that it was not a heart attack. Then the police tried to blame me for murder."

"Oh, I'm sorry. You didn't do it, did you?"

"Of course not," she said indignantly. "I loved my father."

"Do you know who did it?" he asked sincerely.

"The police suspect my mom and her boyfriend. They may be right—insurance money."

"I imagine you must be very upset and angry," he said sincerely. "And I really am sorry for your loss. No wonder you are leaving to start a new life. Do you have a place to live in Albuquerque?"

"With my aunt, at least initially."

"What does your aunt do? Any chance I might know her?"

"She's a lawyer. She works for Johnston, Brown, and Smith. Her name is Kathy Johnston."

"Well, it seems that you and I have something in common. My wife, Brandy, died in an automobile accident about six months ago. The investigators never determined how it happened. The two of us had made this drive for three years to see her son for the holidays, but this year I'm doing it alone. I miss her."

"I miss my father also. He was good to me."

The waitress finally came to take their orders. Debra ordered a T-bone steak with smashed potatoes and carrots, and a glass of merlot.

"I'll have the same," Joey said, "but I'll pass on the wine. Just water."

Then he returned his attention to Debra. "I remember meeting your aunt. I'm in the local chamber of commerce, and I met her at one of our meetings. She's a criminal lawyer, right?"

"I think so."

"Well, we have this business social every month. It's a way for members of the chamber and guests to exchange ideas and business cards and market their products and services to each other. We usually get thirty to fifty attendees. We also have up to three members speak at each meeting. Your aunt spoke at one of our meetings. She impressed me. We spoke briefly and exchanged business cards. If I ever need a criminal lawyer, I wouldn't hesitate to call her. . . So, you'll be living with your aunt?"

"Yes, at least for a while until I pass the nursing exam and get a job."

"Look, my plan was to leave here tomorrow. You're perfectly welcome to ride with me. It will save you the cost of the airline ticket and if this snowstorm is as bad as they think it will be, there may not be a flight out tomorrow either."

"What kind of car are you driving?"

"I'm driving a luxury SUV. Why, does it matter?"

"Well, last time I accepted a ride, it turned out to be a two-seater sports car with a convertible top. It was noisy and bone-jarring."

"Not to worry. My Lexus has plenty of room. It's quiet, and you'll be very comfortable."

She looked right at him. "Okay, I accept your offer, but let me at least pay for the gas."

"You're on."

"What time tomorrow? How will I know when you will be leaving?"

"I hope we can leave in the morning. Depends on the weather. You already have my cell number. It's on my card. Let me have yours. I'll call you in the morning."

"Okay, I'll call you and you'll see it."

They enjoyed their meals and continued to chitchat. Sometime during the meal, she ordered another merlot. He stayed with water.

After they finished eating, they split the bill, but before they got up, Joey said he was curious about something. "I noticed that several people came here with you on the bus. How did the hotel manage to provide everyone with a room?"

"Hmm . . . about that. The hotel didn't have enough rooms, so they have allowed eight of us to camp in one of the meeting rooms. That's where my suitcases and my coat and gloves are."

"What! That's not right!"

"They put me on a list in case a room became available but none did. It's okay. It's only for one night. I'll survive."

"Debra, I have a premium room on the second floor. It has two queen size beds, a large bath with a shower and a heat lamp, a big TV, good cell phone reception, and it's quiet. Please don't misunderstand my intentions when I say this, but you're welcome to share it."

"Hmm . . . I'm not sure. I've had a couple of wines. Can I trust you?"

"I promise I won't take advantage of you and I will respect your privacy. It will be a lot better than trying to sleep on the floor with other people in the room talking, and using an overcrowded public restroom. Tell you what. I've been driving all day. I need to exercise my legs. So, here," he said and handed her a room key. "Take this and check it out. Room 238. Take your time. Freshen up. Relax. Whatever. I'll stay down here for about an hour. When you're done checking it out, give me a call and let me know what you decide."

They rose from their chairs. She quickly slung her saddle bag across her shoulder. She waited for him to put his jacket back on and return his chair to its original position. Then they walked out to the lobby where they parted. She went to the elevators and he went down a hallway to the fitness center.

-4-

BAD NIGHT

Joey entered the fitness center. He and Brandy had made a habit of staying in shape. They even had a Peloton and dumbbells in their house. His body was trim and fit. People who knew him would tell him he looked much younger than his 46 years. The fact that he still had most of his black hair helped. Although not dressed for a strenuous workout, he did have on athletic shoes, so he used the treadmill long enough to simulate a brisk one-mile walk. It was long enough to get the blood circulating in his legs, without getting hot and sweaty. He felt better afterwards.

After that, he walked back to the lobby. An alcove off to the side of the lobby had a TV and cushioned seats. The local news and weather report was on. Several people were in the room standing around the TV listening intently. No one was sitting. *A serious accident on the Interstate— Section of the highway closed—Heavy snow fall expected to last well into the daylight hours—Expected accumulation up to 30 inches.* After hearing the newscast, he felt glad that he had made it to the hotel and was not still on the road. Then he called his stepson Brian to let him know he made it to Flagstaff and about the snowstorm.

He had told Debra she could have an hour. An hour was up and he hadn't heard from her, so he walked back through the lobby and down a hallway to the room with the campers. Perhaps she was there, he thought. He tried the door. It was locked. Only those allowed to be in there could go in, and their belongings would be safe. He peered in through the windows on the double doors. He could see one of the campers nursing a bottle of beer. He didn't see Debra. He turned to leave when two young men came down the hallway talking loudly. One of them carried a small bag. Joey heard him say, "It may be a while before we get a flight out. Good time to party." The other one responded by saying, "All we need now is a willing young chic to join us." They unlocked the door, went inside, and joined their buddy.

Perhaps Debra was still up in his room, he thought. So, he went up. He entered the vestibule and walked past the bathroom into the main room. The room was dimly lit. At the far end of the room near the window he saw Debra sprawled out on the bed. A bed spread covered her body, and a pillow covered the upper part of her head and eyes. Her boots were on the floor next to the bed and her shoulder bag was open and propped up against the wall under the window. She didn't move as he approached. He wondered if she was alive, but then he detected breathing. She was sound asleep!

Being as quiet as he could be, Joey gathered his night clothes and his toiletry bag from his suitcase and took them into the bathroom. He washed up, brushed his teeth, and changed into a pair of black long-legged bottoms and a tight-fitting black polo shirt. He would shower in the morning. What he wore gave the image of an athletic coach. It also accentuated his physical assets. He then tiptoed back into the bedroom, put his underclothes into a white plastic bag, and neatly hung his jacket, shirt, and pants on hangers in the closet. Apparently, he hadn't been that quiet. As he went to his bed, Debra awoke and sat up. Suddenly aware of Joey's presence, she began to apologize profusely.

"Oh my God! I was supposed to call you. I'm sorry! I fell asleep." Then she turned the light on next to her bed and could see Joey more clearly as he stood nearby. She felt a surge of vulnerability as she noticed his tight-fitting top and muscular stature. "**What? You're in your PJs?**" she exclaimed. "I should go." She made it to the edge of the bed and found her boots.

"Debra, please wait! Hear me out. I don't want you to go," he said as he watched her sitting on the edge of her bed struggling to put her boots on.

"Why?"

"I'm concerned about your safety."

"Why?"

"I was just down at the camping room. Three dudes were in there drinking and looking to party. They said that they had everything they needed except for a young chic."

"And you think I would be safer here with you?"

"I do. When I came into my room you were totally out of it. If I wanted to take advantage of you, I would have already done it. You can trust me."

She was looking down toward her feet. "Perhaps it's not you I can't trust," she mumbled, barely loud enough for him to hear.

She looked up, and stared at him, indicating she wanted to hear more.

"I would like you to spend the night here."

"I don't have PJs and I didn't expect to spend the night with a stranger."

"And here I thought we were getting to know each other," he quipped. "It looks like you have an overnight bag with you, and if you are concerned about modesty, I have a robe and a long T-shirt I can lend you."

"Hmm . . . I already have a nightshirt but I will take you up on the robe."

She took her boots back off and grabbed her bag. He handed her the robe as she made her way to the bathroom. "Please turn the light off," she said.

He did as she asked, got into his bed and pulled the covers up over his head. He fell asleep right away and didn't even hear her return from the bathroom.

***

Joey woke up suddenly to blood curdling screams followed by **NO!** . . . **NO!** . . . **NO!** and a long quivering high pitched wail that didn't want to stop. He quickly turned on his light and looked over toward the other bed where the sounds were coming from. Debra was sitting upright in her bed with her hands over her eyes. He could see no explanation other than she was having a bad dream. He instinctively went over to her bed, sat down beside her, and put his arms on her shoulders.

"It's okay, you're safe. It's going to be okay," he said in a tender and caring tone.

She was shaking. She put her arms around him, and pulled herself close. "Dan, I'm sorry, I'm sorry."

He could feel her tears against his cheek as she said this. He wondered who Dan was, but continued his attempt to console her. "Debra, you're just having a bad dream. Wake up."

She reacted and pulled away, looking confused.

"Joey? Oh God," she said. "It seemed so real— Did I just call you Dan? I'm embarrassed."

"It's okay. I've been called worse," he said trying to make light of it. "Do you want to talk about it? They say it helps, and I'm willing to listen."

"Joey, have you ever had nightmares like this?"

"Yes, I do have my own demons. Someone explained to me that our dreams are symbolic exaggerations of reality, and if we can't talk about our experiences and emotions with other people, for whatever reason, we may have nightmares. It's nature's way of cleansing the mind. Having someone to confide in has helped me greatly."

"I don't know if you really want to hear this but I don't think I have much more to lose in terms of your impression of me, so what the hell."

"Don't worry about that."

"I dreamed that my mother came into my bedroom and discovered my father having sex with me. She had a gun, and she was so angry that she shot him through the heart. He fell off the bed and onto the floor. I went to him. Blood was coming out of his mouth. It was a ghastly sight—Was I screaming?"

"Yes, you were. It woke me up. Could I ask you some questions?"

"I guess."

"At dinner you told me that you thought your mother killed him, but it was poison, wasn't it?"

"Yes."

"Was your father named Dan?"

"Yes."

"At dinner, you said the two of you were close and you missed him."

"True."

"Who killed him?"

"I told you. The police think it was my mother and her old boyfriend but they can't prove it."

"Earlier you said they tried to blame you. Why?"

"Mom had kicked Dan out of the house more than a year ago. He had an apartment nearby in Cottonwood, and I often visited him. I had a key and I had access to his food and medicine."

"And why did your mother kick Dan out of the house?"

"Uh . . . they didn't get along."

"Sounds like it was more than that. Did she hate him enough to kill him?"

"Uh . . ."

He sensed that she was holding something back.

"It's okay if you're not ready to answer that question. You don't have to, although it might help." But he could see she was not ready to do so. "Maybe we should try to get some sleep. We may have to dig out before we get back on the road tomorrow. Look, for what's its worth, I don't have a bad impression of you. It took courage for you to talk about this. Will you be okay if I turn off the light?"

"Yes, thank you for helping me." She laid back down.

He went back to his bed and turned off the light.

-5-

DIGGING OUT

Joey woke up early the next morning. He showered, dressed and repacked. As he was about to go downstairs, Debra woke up. He told her she could take her time and meet him downstairs in the restaurant for breakfast, when she was ready. He was eager to check on the status of the snowstorm. He walked down to the lobby and out the main entrance to investigate. It didn't look good. Snow was still falling. He looked over at the parking lot where he remembered parking his car. White forms filled the lot, barely resembling the cars underneath. He watched as a maintenance vehicle plowed the pavement between the rows of cars—piling more snow up behind each parking space in the process. Until the maintenance crew finished plowing, it would be futile to start shoveling out the car. And speaking of a shovel, he had a small shovel in the trunk, but it would take a while to even get the trunk opened. Perhaps the hotel had a few shovels that people could borrow, he thought. He went back inside and talked to the manager on duty. He said they would see what they could do. Then he asked if he could extend his reservation for another night if necessary. The manger told him yes, but he would need to let him know for sure by 11 a.m. In the meantime, he was hungry. He called Debra. She said she was just getting out of the shower and would be down in a few minutes. He took a morning paper, found a comfortable chair in the lobby, and began to do the crossword while he waited.

Debra came down fifteen minutes later. He waived and she came to where he was sitting.

"I'm sorry. I took longer than I expected. Did you check outside? What does it look like?"

"Come. You can see for yourself."

They walked out the main entrance to the edge of the parking lot.

"It's still snowing?"

Then she looked toward the parking area.

"Oh my God. Where's your car?"

"Good question."

"Will we have to stay another night?"

"As much as I enjoy rooming with you, I'm going to do my best to get us out of here. However, I did take the liberty of arranging to stay another night if necessary. But, right now, I think we should get some breakfast."

After a hearty breakfast, they began the job of digging out. Joey was able to borrow a shovel from the hotel. He got a crazy look when he went to pick it up.

A hotel employee was already outside trying to clear as much snow and ice as possible from the hotel entranceway. Joey and Debra went into the parking area and began shoveling snow from the rear of a car he thought was his. He would know for sure once he exposed the license plate. Debra was right there with him using her hands to move as much snow as possible. Then she paused.

"Joey, I have an idea. I'll be back shortly." She returned three minutes later with a metal wastepaper can, and began scooping up snow and dumping it away from the car.

"Very clever idea," he told her. "Where did you find the can?"

"You don't want to know," she responded. He chuckled to himself.

They began removing snow from the rear of the car. Finally, they could see the blue color of the car body and then the plate and Lexus emblem. It was his car. He began removing snow from above the cargo door. His next objective was to be able to open it. Debra began removing snow from the driver's side of the car. Meanwhile a utility truck with two workers drove up the driveway to the hotel and turned into the parking area. One of them walked over to them.

"You're probably wasting your time," he said. "Roads are still impassable and they expect another six inches before noontime. Wind gust are still high and the on-ramps to Interstate Forty remain closed due to conditions and a chain pile up."

"Just curious," Joey responded. "How did you guys manage to get here?"

"We didn't have very far to go. Our facility building is just up the road. We also have large wheels and chains on our tires."

"Well, I appreciate your input. I hadn't realized it was that bad, but I figured I'd get a head start on digging out."

Debra was listening and turned to Joey with a questioning look. He walked over to her.

"It might take another two hours to get the car free, but I think it would be worth doing that, even if we don't go anywhere."

"Joey, what time do we need to check out?"

"Eleven; it's ten now. We can dig for another hour and then decide what we're going to do."

"Okay."

Forty-five minutes later they had made progress and Joey was able to get into the driver's seat, start the engine and dislodge the car enough to move it a foot backwards. They were far from done. Snow still packed the passenger side of the car and covered the roof, and at least a foot of snow remained behind the car. It was still windy and cold, and the sun was not out, but the good news was that the snow had stopped falling, at least for now.

"Joey, let's talk. I don't think we should check out. Even if we finally get the car on the road, I'm not sure driving on these roads is a good idea."

"Yeah, you're right. I guess I was overly optimistic, but I agree. Debra, are you okay with sharing the room again?"

"I am if you are," she quickly responded. He was surprised at her lack of hesitation, but pleased.

"I promised the front desk I would let them know." They started back to the lobby when a couple walked out toward them. They stopped in their tracks when they saw the mounds of snow before them.

Joey greeted them. "Good morning. Some mess huh?"

"How will we ever get out of here?" the woman asked.

"Well, you can use our tools," Joey said as he offered the shovel and the wastebasket. "They belong to the hotel, so we don't need them back. We're taking a break and will return this afternoon, but I got into my car and I have my own shovel in there."

"Isn't there a service that can shovel us out?" the woman asked.

"Don't know. Do you need to leave right away?"

"We had hoped to."

"Same here, but it looks like tomorrow is more realistic. Perhaps we'll see you later."

Joey and Debra proceeded to the front desk and verified that they had a reservation for one more night. They retrieved Debra's suitcases from the camper room and took them to Joey's room upstairs. They had a small lunch in the dining room and then it was back to the parking lot.

"Joey, that woman asked if there were some workers who would dig out our cars for us. Have you considered that?"

"Yeah, I did. I asked at the front desk this morning. The problem is no one could get here and they are short on staff. But we have more time now. We should be okay. Come on, let's go have some fun in the snow." He formed a snow ball. "Here catch," he said and lobbed the snow ball at her.

She laughed. "So, you want to play, do you?" Her returned fire was more than a lob and hit him mid-chest.

"Good arm."

"High school softball team."

He fired back. "College baseball team."

She grabbed a pile of snow, made a crude snowball and ran toward him, pasting the snow on the side of his face. "Take that mister."

He had no choice. He made his own snowball and chased her to the embankment on the edge of the parking lot. As he pasted her, she fell backwards onto the snowbank pulling him down on top of her. They gazed into each other's eyes. They had a "moment" but quickly recovered their senses and got up.

They went over to the Lexus. He retrieved a snow brush and scrapper and handed it to her. He retrieved the shovel for himself. They worked for more than an hour. When the car was free of all snow and ice, they congratulated each other with high fives and laughter.

They were both tuckered out. Back in the hotel room, they napped, on separate beds of course.

With nowhere else to go, they had supper in the Skyway Bar and Grill once again. She ordered the chicken plate with a glass of white wine and he had the same, but without the wine. They talked about sports and about her home town.

She told him that her father's family had an estate in Cornville. She grew up there and graduated from high school in nearby Cottonwood.

"You told me earlier you were on your school softball team."

"I was. I was also on the swimming team."

"So, you're athletic. And you didn't seem to mind helping me shovel my car out. Do you enjoy outdoor activities?"

"I do. Besides sports, I also enjoy hiking, bike riding and I've even learned to ride a horse. We had horses on our property when I was young. Unfortunately, I haven't had as much time to do these things recently. We didn't have a lot of money growing up. In the summer of my junior and senior years, I worked at the Cottonwood Medical Center. Then I worked in the medical center in Sedona while getting my BSN degree from NAU in Flagstaff."

"How old did you say you were?" Joey asked.

"I didn't. I'll be twenty-two at the end of this month."

"And you already have a bachelor's degree?"

"Did it in three years but that included summers— mostly online."

"You must be very smart."

"Yup, didn't you notice?" she said jokingly. "No, not really— I'm just a hard worker."

"Now Joey you need to tell me more about yourself. Your business card said you are the Vice President of Operations. That sounds very impressive."

"Not really. It's a small company and I've been there for ten years now. Until four years ago I was the marketing manager."

"What does your company actually do?"

"We sell a service. Clients hire us to advise them on what types of security they need, and then if they choose, we manage the project to implement it."

"And what are your responsibilities?"

"Marketing, consulting, and project management. Like I said we're small so I only have seven people under me. They each have unique skills so we pretty much work as a team. My boss, Frank Wilson, handles the financial, accounting, legal and personnel aspects of the company. He's also the company CEO and has the biggest share of company ownership. I own a small portion." He was pleased that she seemed to be paying attention to what he was saying.

"Do you like your boss?" She asked.

"I do. In fact, we're friends. We play golf together. He and his wife had dinner with us a few times. We get along very well. Why do you ask?"

"Well, my dad had a job once where he didn't like his boss, and he was out of a job because of it. My mom was angry at him. He told Mom that his boss asked him to do something that was not ethical, so he quit. Mom said that sometimes you need to do things you don't like."

"Well, what your mom said is true up to a point, but at some point, you need to draw the line. It's not always easy to know when, so I can't blame your dad."

After supper, they both made calls on their cell phones. After calling her friend in Cottonwood, Debra called her Aunt Kay and told her that she would need to spend one more night in Flagstaff due to the snowstorm. "Yes," she said to her aunt, "I am still riding home with Joey Ramirez. We spent most of the day digging out his car." Of course, she made no mention that they were sharing a room. Meanwhile, Joey called his secretary at work. He left a message that he was still snowbound. He would not be returning to work for another day, and to please reschedule any appointments. Then Joey and Debra went to the fitness center and exercised their legs for several minutes before heading up to the room.

-6-

TAKING IT TO A NEW LEVEL

Debra was first into the bathroom to wash up and change into her night clothes. Joey waited his turn in a cushioned easy chair in the corner near the window. Several minutes later, he watched her come out, scamper across the room and plop herself atop her bed. Apparently, she had lost the shyness she had the night before. Not that there was anything indecent about what she wore—a knee length flannel night shirt and winter socks, but no robe. Now it was Joey's turn in the bathroom. He changed into his PJs, as she had called them the night before, returned to the easy chair and turned on the floor lamp. He began working on the crossword that he had started in the morning while waiting for her to come downstairs. Several minutes of silence followed. Every now and then he would look up as he contemplated the possible answers to one of the clues. Once when he did so, he noticed Debra in a rather suggestive position. She had her knees bent up revealing the upper parts of her thighs. Naturally, that aroused him. Although he thought the better of it, he couldn't stop gazing. Somehow, she caught him looking, or so he thought. He expected her to be angry, but she just looked at him and smiled. Perhaps she hadn't noticed, so he took the initiative.

"Uh, Debra, what are you reading?"

"It's a woman's magazine. There's an article on ways to make yourself more attractive to the opposite sex. Joey in your opinion, do you think I'm attractive?" As she said this, she slowly straightened her legs, eliminating the suggestive view.

He figured he better think carefully before he answered. She had attracted his attention when he first met her, and she had aroused him just now. Otherwise, he hadn't given her physical appearance much thought. She was about five foot, six inches tall, not too heavy, not too thin. At dinner, her flannel shirt hid the true size of her breasts and her night shirt was too loose fitting to reveal her true shape. But she was smart, he liked her personality, and she had a clear complexion and a pretty face.

"I do find you attractive," he finally said.

"Do you think I should wear makeup?"

"Well, of course I've never seen you with makeup, and I think you are attractive without it. You have well-balanced facial features and natural beauty. For what it's worth, I personally like you just the way you are."

"Hmm . . . in the article they also talk about how men are attracted to women who reveal more of their body. Joey . . . I know you were looking at me a few moments ago. Did you like what you saw?"

So, she had noticed. He was embarrassed, but didn't want to show it. He arose from his chair, went over to her, and sat on the side of her bed.

"Debra, I really like you, and I've enjoyed every minute that I've been with you. And, to be honest, you do turn me on."

"Joey, I like you too. So, what's holding you back?"

"When you agreed to share a room with me you seemed very hesitant. I promised I would respect you and that I wouldn't take advantage of you. I've tried very hard to keep my promise."

"You don't need to keep your promise anymore," she said softly.

She put her arm around his neck and pulled him to her. They kissed tenderly but briefly. "I want you to make love to me Joey."

"Debra, I don't want this to be a one-night stand. I like you too much for that. I want to see you again after we get to Albuquerque. I don't want to get you pregnant either."

"It's not likely. I just finished my period two days ago." He believed her; he had noticed a used tampon in the bathroom the previous night. He gave in to her wishes.

"Lie back," he said softly. He lifted her nightshirt, removed her panties, and kissed every part of her body before he entered her and brought her to climax. Afterwards they got under the covers and held each other tightly.

-7-

ON THE ROAD AGAIN

The next morning, they were up early, eager to get on the road. They got themselves together, had a small breakfast, loaded the car, and checked out of the hotel. It was only eight in the morning when they drove off. The good news was that the snow had stopped falling, and the wind had died down. Joey's first job was to get gas and then find his way to Interstate 40. It took more than half an hour. Plows were still working to clear the roads. Even on the Interstate, for the first 50 miles they could only average about 45 miles per hour due to plows and lane closures. But after that, the sun came out, the Interstate became clear, and the driving got easier.

Earlier the two of them had been focusing on packing, checking out, and the weather, and Joey had been focusing on his driving. They hadn't said much to each other and Joey thought Debra seemed extra quiet and moody. But now that the driving got easier, Joey turned his attention to Debra. He wondered if she was having regrets about what they did the night before. She had put the seat back and seemed relaxed, but her eyes were open, so he began talking to her.

"Debra, you've been very quiet this morning. Is everything okay?"

"I'm fine," she responded in a tone that told Joey that she wasn't fine."

"Do you want to talk about last night?"

"I'm not sure."

"If you regret that it happened, or think it was a mistake, you can say so."

"I'm concerned that maybe *you* think that. I know that I encouraged you, and you seemed to enjoy it, but maybe you didn't mean to give in. And I'm worried that maybe you will think less of me for it."

"I don't think less of you. I really meant it when I said I didn't want a one-night stand. But if that's what *you* want, you should tell me."

"It's not what I want. I like you."

"Then *what*?"

"I'm thinking about everything in my life that lies ahead—a lot of unknowns. I'm wondering if I'll have time for a relationship."

"I can understand that. I know you have a lot on your plate. You need to settle into your new home with your aunt, and you need to pass your nursing exam and start a new career. Those things *should* be your primary concern right now. I'm not going to pressure you. Thing is, I like you too, but if you tell me that you just want to be friends, I can accept that as well."

"I don't want to just be friends, but can we take it slowly?"

"Absolutely. I'll let you take the lead. Whenever you need me, say so and I'll be here for you."

"Thanks for understanding. I really do like you . . . but I'd like to know more about you."

"Okay. What would you like to know?"

"Joey, you mentioned your stepson. And you visited him in California. Didn't he live with you and your wife?"

"No. Brian is older than you. Has a wife and a little boy. Left home before I married Brandy."

"How long were you and Brandy married?"

"Only three years, and seven weeks."

"I see, and were you married before?"

"Nope."

"So, you have no kids of your own?"

"Nope. Unfortunately, I don't."

"So, . . . why not? Sounds like you wish you did."

"Yeah, and I still have that wish, but so far things haven't panned out. I've focused on my career. Until I met Brandy, I never found someone I wanted to have a family with. Unfortunately, after she had Brian and divorced her husband, she decided she didn't want to get pregnant again. She didn't believe in abortion, so she had her tubes tied. That's why Brandy and I couldn't have kids together."

"Joey, how old are you?"

"Forty-six," he answered truthfully.

"You look much younger," she told him. "Your wish might still come true."

"Thanks for the compliment," he replied. "Okay if I turn on some music? What kind of music would you like?"

"Something relaxing works for me. Yesterday tired me out, but then I didn't sleep well last night. I was uptight about things, but I feel more relaxed now that we talked."

He tuned into some soft satellite music; Debra closed her eyes and fell asleep.

At around noon, they got off the Interstate for a small lunch.

Before they were back on the road, Debra took the opportunity to call Aunt Kay to let her know where they were.

"Joey. Kay says hello. She wants to know when she could expect us and where we can meet."

"You can tell her that we expect to be at the intersection of Interstate 40 and Interstate 25 in about three hours—about four o'clock. Tell her I'm willing to take you all the way to her house, but I'll need directions."

Debra relayed his reply, and then a seemingly long time passed, before giving Joey an update.

"Aunt Kay says she lives in the Enchanted Park area off Menaul Boulevard. She wants to know if you live in the Embudo Canyon area."

"I do, why?"

"She just found out she may need to be in court this afternoon and doesn't know when she will be home—could be as late as seven. She also said she doesn't leave a spare key under the mat. She says her house is not far from where you live, and wants to know if it would be okay if she picks me up at your house. She will call first."

"I'm okay with that. Ask her if she would like the three of us to have a take-out supper when she arrives. I can order it when she calls and it will be ready by the time she arrives."

Debra and Kay talk for a few moments and then click off.

"Aunt Kay says she can pick it up on the way to your house. We can decide details when she calls. She looks forward to seeing you."

"I'm looking forward to seeing her as well. I'd like to know more about her."

"Well, she's my dad's sister and she's almost like a second mother to me. She's visited us in Arizona several times over the years. When I was young, she would always bring me a small present, and I'd run out to meet her and give her a hug. Although we never went to visit her—don't know why, except maybe money had something to do with it. We didn't have much, and there was a period when my dad was out of work. She helped us out, and more recently she's paid my tuition for nursing school."

"Sounds like she's doing alright for herself. Was she married? Any kids?"

"I think she was married once and divorced. Obviously kept her name, but it was before my time. Dad never talked much about that."

As they arrived on the outskirts of Albuquerque a few minutes before four, traffic began to slow.

"We're now crossing the Rio Grande," he proudly announced. "On the right you can see the Old Town and the Downtown areas of Albuquerque. Your aunt probably works somewhere over there on the east side of Downtown," he said. "That's where the courts and the legal offices are."

"Is Old Town the original city?"

"Well, they have determined that indigenous people lived here as far back as twelve thousand years ago. But the Spanish established Old Town in 1706 as a trading post. Later, after New Mexico became part of the United States, the railroad came and built a railroad station in the area that became Downtown—We're now approaching the intersection of Interstate 40 and Interstate 25. We're right on schedule."

"Do you live very far from here?"

"See those hills and the mountain range ahead of us and to our left? That's the Sandia Range. I live right up against the foothills. He gestured with his left arm as he spoke. Your aunt lives a tad to the north and slightly back in this direction. It could take us another half hour or more to get to my place, depending on traffic."

"Wow, it's really spread out. Is all that part of Albuquerque?"

"It is. Albuquerque includes four counties."

"How many people live here?"

"They estimate just under nine hundred thousand. But it's hard to know for sure because there are an unknown number of unregistered immigrants. You're going to find that Albuquerque is more integrated than Cottonwood. About forty-five percent of the population here is Latino. Only about forty percent is white."

"Joey, are you Latino?"

"I'm half Latino. I was born in Texas. My father was from Central America and my birth mother was from Texas and white. What about you? Your skin seems tan like mine."

"Don't know. I don't know anything about my birth parents. Until recently, my mom wanted me to think she was my birth mother. I think my dad knew who they were, but Mom wouldn't let him tell me."

"You ever try to find out?"

"I made some feeble attempts to do so but ran into roadblocks. Apparently, I'm not legally allowed to see my own original birth certificate. Doesn't seem fair."

"No, it doesn't. I agree."

-8-

HOME

They arrived at Joey's house around four-thirty. He pulled into his short driveway and stopped in front of the two-car garage. As they walked to the front door, Debra was taking it all in.

"Very interesting. Much different than out in the country where I'm from. The lots here are so much smaller and the houses are all close together." He didn't take her comment as an insult. He was learning that she called things as they were, and he liked that about her.

"Well, it's different, but you get used to it. This community is more upscale than most. Brandy and I purchased it in two thousand twelve when we married. As you can see, the houses in this community are all different—customized. We made improvements to it before we moved in. Its value has appreciated considerably. Let's go in and I'll give you a tour."

They walked into a short vestibule and stopped at the security panel. Joey punched in a code and they proceeded into a spacious living room to the right. Debra noticed a staircase to the left. "That goes up to a master bedroom and bath above the garage," he said.

Then they proceeded to an open dining area to the rear of the living room. He opened the drapes on the other side of the dining area revealing sliding glass doors. "The sliding glass doors go out to a deck that runs the length of the house. We'll walk out there later. The kitchen is on the left, and the hallway to the right leads to two bedrooms and another bathroom." He walked her down the hallway. "I turned this bedroom into an office that I shared with Brandy. And here at the end of the hallway is a large guest bedroom. It has direct access to the bathroom and to the deck. Have a look. What do you think?"

"Nice!" she responded noticing the twin beds at one end of the room and the doors to the deck at the other end. Do you have many guests?"

"Not so much, now that Brandy's gone."

"Seems like a big house for just you. Have you considered selling?"

"Well, I don't know. It's kind of lonely by myself, but otherwise I like it here, and property values are still increasing, so I'm in no hurry. Let me show you the kitchen."

She followed him back past the dining area and into the kitchen.

"Wow! Your kitchen is nice," she said as her eyes surveyed the modernized kitchen design with all the latest appliances.

"You seem surprised."

"My mom's house in Cornville is very old. Your kitchen is much more modern than hers. It looks brighter and cheerier too. Your wife must have really liked it."

He chuckled. "Well, she did, but I did most of the cooking."

"Oh, really. You must be good at it."

"Well, I can't say I'm that good at it, but my skill has improved over the years. . . Come let me show you the rest of the house."

They went back to the dining area and proceeded through the sliding glass doors onto the deck.

"This is nice. I like the mountain view," she said.

"There are trails out there that are easy to get to. Brandy and I were bikers and we often rode together. Have you ridden one?"

"Uh, a bike?" obviously not sure of what he meant.

He smiled. "I'm talking motorcycles, not bicycles."

"No. I've never been on one."

"Well, if you are interested, you can ride on the back of mine and we can tour the hills."

"Okay, I might take you up on that." She grinned.

"You know, we could ride up to the Sandia Tramway and take the Tram up to the peak—more than ten thousand feet up. The view is incredible, and it's open year-round. It's a must for anyone who comes to Albuquerque. How about Saturday?"

"Joey, I'd really like to do this with you, but I don't know what my schedule is going to be. I will need to pass my registered nursing exam, and apply for a nursing license in this state. And, in the meantime I need to find a job, short term and long term. And then, I'm not sure what Aunt Kay might have in store for me."

"Yes, of course. I understand. I don't want to pressure you. Launching your career should be your top priority, and it's also important that you establish a good relationship with your aunt. I don't want to stand in the way of that. Debra, I would like to help you anyway I can. I don't know if this will help, but I told you I'm well-known in the Chamber of Commerce, and my company has provided services to a medical clinic and to one of the local hospitals. I could talk to them to see if they have job openings and if nothing else, I could certainly write you a favorable recommendation."

"You would do that?"

"Absolutely! Debra, maybe an ongoing relationship with me is not in your best interest right now, I get that, but I want you to know that I care about you. If you need me, just say the word. I'm here for you."

"Joey, I care about you too, and I will make time for us." She put her hands aside his head and pulled it down to her, planting a firm kiss on his mouth in the process. Then she quickly pulled away. "I'd like to see the rest of your house."

"Would you like to see the lower level?"

"Lead the way."

They descended a staircase from the kitchen that led down to the lower level.

"This was an unfinished basement before we moved in. Because we're on a slope, the front of the basement is below the ground, and the rear opens to the outside. We enlarged the doorway to the outside and we added a room that I use for storage. As you can see most of the area is a bar and recreation room. We used it for entertaining friends and clients, watching sports on the large screen TV, and—"

"Wow, a pool table!" she exclaimed. "Can we play?"

"You play?" he asked with a look of surprise.

"My dad taught me. Much to the chagrin of my mom, he bought a table and installed it in a refurbished section of our house. Mom thought it was a waste of money. Dad played regularly on a team at local bars as well. Anyway, he taught me how to play."

"Rack em up. Let's see what you've got."

She was good. They played for over an hour before the phone rang. Aunt Kay was leaving work.

As agreed, Joey called in an order for ribs and coleslaw, family style, more than enough for the three of them. He paid with a credit card. Aunt Kay would pick up the order along the way there.

Thirty minutes later Joey met her at the door with Debra right behind.

"Pleased to see you. I'm Joseph Ramirez. Just call me Joey. Let me take that," he said, as he took the food bag and took it into the kitchen.

Debra and Aunt Kay then greeted each other with a warm embrace and followed Joey to the kitchen.

"Joey, I want to thank you for helping Debra to find a way home."

"Not a problem. Should I call you Aunt Kay?" Joey asked.

"My professional name is Kathy Johnston, but you may call me Kay," she told him. "I think we may have met once before."

"Yes, I think it was at a chamber event, three years ago at the Sandia Resort. I would have given you my business card."

"I think that was it."

"You said you live nearby?"

"I live in the Enchanted Park area, no more than a mile away, just north of Menaul Boulevard."

"You're a lawyer, right? Where did you say you worked?"

"I work for Johnston, Brown, and Smith. Our offices are located on Louisiana Boulevard, just south of Menaul, so I can follow Menaul Boulevard, almost all the way from work."

"How do you find the traffic? Does it take you long to get to work?"

"Depends on the time of day. It can take as long as forty-five minutes. How about you?"

"Our offices are in a business park on Innovation Parkway, near Sandia Labs. Takes less than half an hour in the morning."

"Do you still sell security systems?"

"No, no. Our primary business is security system *consulting*, *design*, and *project management*. We don't deal, sell, or resell for any vendor. Don't want to get technical, but for us it's an important distinction."

They preceded to the dining area and Joey set the table while Debra showed Aunt Kay where to wash up. When they returned, Debra mentioned that Aunt Kay had dressed for court and wondered if Joey had an apron.

"Yes," Joey responded. His eyes scanned the dressy blouse and slacks she wore in court. They went well with her tan skin and black hair, he thought. He could not help but notice her shapely figure as well. "Your aunt looks too nice to be covered with rib sauce. This should cover her entire torso," he said so that Kay could overhear, and offered a full shoulder to knee apron.

"Thank you," Kay said, appreciative of the attention. The chitchat continued as they ate.

"Joey, you have a very nice house. Have you been here long?"

"About three and a half years. Just after I got married."

"Oh, that's right. She passed away . . . about six months ago, wasn't it? It was in the paper. I'm sorry for your loss. How are you handling it?"

"I'm adjusting."

"As a lawyer, I was interested in the case and I read the news articles. They said they hadn't determined the exact cause of death but it looked suspicious. They cleared you but were looking for the good Samaritan who pulled her out of the car before it went up in flames. Did they ever find him?"

"Ah, no, they never did," he said before intentionally changing the subject. "So, Debra tells me you bought her a car."

Aunt Kay turned her head toward Debra as she spoke. "Ha-ha. Doesn't she wish? No, I bought *myself* a car for her to *use*. As soon as she gets a job, she can buy it from me."

Debra opened her mouth as if to speak but Joey spoke first. "What model car is it?"

"It's a year-old Kia. It's good on gas. It's the car I drove up in."

"Well, it's hard to do without a car around here. Debra, you're lucky to have Kay as your aunt."

"Yes, I know that, and Aunt Kay, I am very appreciative. Thank you."

The evening lasted until nine o'clock. As Kay walked out, she thanked Joey for the hospitality and said she hoped to see him again. As Debra followed, he spoke softly in her ear.

"You can text me. Let me know how you're doing, okay?"

She acknowledged with a smile and, "I will."

-9-

SATURDAY VISITS

The following Friday evening, Joey was pleasantly surprised to receive a text on his cell phone from Debra.

"I need you. May I come to your place? 9 a.m.?"
He responded immediately. *"Yes. 9 OK."*

He hadn't heard from her since Monday, so he wondered why she suddenly needed him, but he would know soon enough.

He was up early the next morning, had breakfast, and made himself presentable. The day was sunny and warm, already 50 degrees when Debra arrived at ten past nine. When he let her in, she gave him a tight embrace, put her arms around his neck and kissed him hard. He thought for sure she wanted to make love so he began to undo her blouse and kiss her neck.

"No Joey, not yet. I need to talk to you first."

"Okay, what's going on? Talk to me." They took a seat on the living room sofa and turned towards each other to talk.

"I need to talk to you about Aunt Kay. After we got home Monday, she told me how much she liked you. I mean she was gushing. Said she wanted to get to know you better. I wasn't sure how to respond, but told her I liked you too. Then she told me that when she met you three years ago at the chamber event, she singled you out because she found you to be handsome and attractive. She confessed that she was hoping to initiate a relationship with you until someone informed her that you were happily married. And now of course she knows you aren't any more. She told me that she would like to invite you to go out to dinner with me to celebrate my birthday. She was thinking Saturday, a couple of weeks from now. She wanted to know what I thought of the idea. Again, I didn't know how to answer, and told her I would let her know."

"Does she know you're here now?"

"Yes. I told her about the pool table and that you said I could come anytime to use it. She knows I play, and agreed that playing here would be a lot safer than at some of the bars in the area. I also told her you were helping me find job opportunities and that you had one you wanted to talk to me about that. Those were white lies, I know. But she said maybe I could ask you about the birthday dinner idea, and if you were interested, she would call you and work out the details with you."

"So, what are you going to tell her?"

"Joey, I was hoping you would help me with that," she said excitedly. "The two of you seemed to hit it off quite well the other night. I need to know how you feel about it. I need to know if you are as interested in her as she seems to be in you."

"Ah, Oh. Sorry. I understand now. I'm just a little slow on the uptake." He thought for moment, trying to find the right words. "Debra, the way I like you is different than the way I like her. Sharing a bed is not the same as sharing membership in the Chamber of Commerce. You and I have an emotional bond based on things we've experienced. I don't have that with your aunt and I don't want to. And yet, if we continue to see each other, I think it's important that I not snub her. Okay, so what can we do?"

"Yeah, that's the question."

"I think I should accept the dinner invitation." He held up his hand as he saw Debra about to protest. "The burden is on me to let her know that I want to be friends, but that I'm not interested in being intimate with her. At some point however, if you and I are still together, and I hope we are, we will need to let her know about us."

"You may be right," she responded.

"Did she indicate where she wanted to go for your birthday?"

"No. I think she wanted to get some input from you."

"I see. Well, if it was just the two of us, I would ask you to go to the Moonlight Lounge at the Sandia Resort. It's kind of up to her though, isn't it? She should call me. We can talk."

"Joey, I still need you," she said softly.

"I need you too. Let's go down the hall."

Before they engaged, Joey brought up the subject of birth control. He was aware of her cycle and he didn't want to get her pregnant.

"Debra, I don't think you want me to get you pregnant. Would you mind if I use a condom?"

Her reply surprised him. She pulled something out of her purse and held it up before him. "I already thought of that," she said and handed him a condom.

They went down the hallway to the guest bedroom. After an hour of pleasure, they talked.

"I want you to know something," he said. "When you told Kay that I would help you to find a job that was not a white lie. I do know someone that will be looking for a nurse. He's going to open a new clinic in two or three months from now. He's not ready to hire anyone right now, and you don't have your credentials yet, but it won't hurt to talk with him and be first in line when you are both ready. I will give you his contact information and you can call him and tell him I referred you. I will also let him know that you may be contacting him, if that's okay."

"Oh Joey, thank you. I really appreciate you."

"And I invite you to play pool here so long as you call first. So that was not a white lie either."

"Can we play after we wash up?"

"You're on, and I'm not going to let you win," he boasted.

After they left the guest bedroom and washed up, they played three racks of eight-ball. It was close but Joey beat her two out of three. Then Joey made them lunch. When they parted, they agreed to see each other again the following Saturday.

The following Saturday morning, they repeated the activity of the prior week—talk, sex, pool, and lunch.

-10-

BIRTHDAY DINNER

Kay called Joey the next day on Sunday after she returned from church. They worked out the details for Debra's birthday dinner. Debra's birthday was Tuesday, January 26, but they had agreed to celebrate the preceding Saturday evening, less than a week away. They decided to go to a fine Mexican restaurant and night spot on Montgomery Boulevard called El Palacio Latino. In addition to fine Mexican cuisine, on Saturday nights they had a Latino combo and a dance floor. Kay had been to the El Palacio on several occasions and considered it an ideal place to develop a relationship with Joey. Joey said he knew where it was and he would meet them there at seven o'clock.

Kathy (Kay) Johnston was 38 years old. She was single and had given up hope of a successful marriage with children years ago. What she did have was a successful career, good looks, and money. From time to time, she had enjoyable relationships with men she encountered in the business world or at church. She looked forward to knowing Joey.

The night before they were to meet at La Palacio, Joey sent a special text and E-card to Debra wishing her a happy birthday. She responded by thanking him for the cute greeting and that she looked forward to tomorrow evening. She also said that Aunt Kay seemed to be looking forward to it even more. Joey understood her subtle inference.

El Palacio was a one-story sand colored stucco-faced structure. Except for the sign over the main entrance, one could mistake it for a professional office building. Joey arrived five minutes early and waited in the lobby for Debra and Kay. They arrived shortly. A hostess promptly sat them at a table for three, with easy access to, and a good view of, the dance floor. Musical instruments already sat on a platform behind the dance floor awaiting the 8:30 arrival of Los Cuatro Amigos.

"This seems like a very nice place," Debra said as she looked at Joey. "Aunt Kay says she's been here many times and likes it. Have you been here before?"

He smiled. "Yes, I have, a couple of times. I hope you enjoy it."

Several other parties were there for dinner, and a couple of people sat at a bar off to the side of the dining area. The waitress came promptly after the hostess had seated them. Debra and Kay each ordered a glass of white wine and Joey ordered a Shirley Temple. His order earned him a strange glance from Kay. Soon after their drinks arrived the waitress came to take their food order. Joey remembered that they liked to have all the food ordered before the entertainment and dancing began. Joey took the opportunity to say something to the waitress in Spanish. After a short conversation the waitress glanced at Debra, smiled and left.

"I'm impressed," Kay gushed. "How did you become so fluent in Spanish?"

"My father spoke Spanish and after he divorced my birth mother, he married my stepmother who was from Mexico," It was a white lie, but he figured it would suffice.

While they continued the banter over drinks, an attractive middle-aged Latino lady approached their table.

"Señor Ramirez? Do you remember me? It has been a long time." She spoke with a definite Spanish accent.

Joey, politely stood and greeted her in Spanish. *"Señora, buenas noches."*

The woman turned to face Debra and Kay, and introduced herself. "I'm Señora Sanchez. I was Mister Joey's dance instructor, well him and his wife, before they married. . . Oh I heard she passed. I'm so sorry," she said to Joey. "I hope you're holding up okay. Are you?"

"I'm doing fine. Thanks for asking."

She turned and looked at Kay. "Joey was my favorite student. He didn't need much training though. He was already an excellent dancer when I first met him."

Kay's interest perked up when she heard this. "I'm learning all kinds of new things about you Joey."

"Señora, let me introduce you," Joey offered. "These are my friends, Kay and Debra Johnston. We're celebrating Debra's birthday tonight."

"How nice. Pleased to meet you both. Well, I need to get back to my table. I wish you a happy birthday Debra. I hope you and your mother enjoy the evening, and it was especially nice seeing you again Joey. They're having Latino dance music tonight. I expect to see you on the dance floor," she said. Joey was about to correct her understanding of the relationship between Debra and Kay, but he wasn't quick enough. She had already turned to leave.

Joey sat back down and the three of them enjoyed a very good Mexican style meal. Afterwards, the waitress brought a special surprise for Debra—a generous cube of Mexican *pastel de tres leches*, with a candle on top. She shared it with everyone. Meanwhile the band began playing, and Joey had his eyes fixed on the dance floor. A few couples were already dancing.

Kay saw her opportunity. "Joey, I'm probably not as good a dancer as you, but would you like to dance? Perhaps you could teach me a step or two," she quipped.

Joey hesitated and looked at Debra. "Debra, would you mind?"

"Why would she mind?" Kay asked.

"It's fine. Enjoy," Debra responded with a slight tone of resignation.

Joey and Kay danced while Debra watched. Debra watched her Aunt Kay ask Joey for guidance, after which she seemed to know exactly what to do. She watched her missteps become excuses for incidental physical contact. And Joey seemed to be enjoying it. Debra's heart sank. When they returned to the table, Aunt Kay had her arm around Joey's waist, and they were laughing.

"That was fun," Kay said. "Thank you."

"Yes, the two of you dance very well together. I'm envious," Debra said.

"I'd like to dance with you, Debra. Will you join me?"

"Joey, I've never danced to Latino music and I would embarrass you . . . and myself."

"You sure?"

"Well, if you don't want to Debra, I sure want to," Kay offered.

He looked at Debra, and sensed that she was not happy. "Kay would it be okay if I pass on that? Maybe we should pay the bill and take a walk outside, instead."

"While you and Aunt Kay are settling, I'm going to the lady's room. I'll meet you at the front door."

After they took care of the bill, Kay went to the ladies' room and Joey went to the front door to find Debra. He found her sitting on the bench. She seemed to have tears in her eyes. He sat close and put his arm around her.

"What's wrong?"

"Nothing," she mumbled.

"Debra, please talk to me."

"You and Aunt Kay. She's all over you and you seem to love it. At first, I thought I was jealous, but then I began to think maybe I'm just not in your league. Maybe, I'm too young and inexperienced. Maybe she has more of what you need."

"Debra, stop. It's not true. Please don't feel that way. You're exactly what I need. I'm in love with *you*—"

His words got her attention, but before he could finish his sentence, Kay returned from the ladies' room and Debra pulled away.

"What's going on with you two? Debra, are you alright?"

Joey and Debra stood up. "I'm fine. Just tired," she said and tried to hide her tears.

Kay looked at Joey. "I was going to invite you to follow us to my house for—"

"I appreciate the offer, but I think I should call it a night. I'm kind of tired myself."

Kay looked confused. "Something I should know?"

"I think you and Debra should talk."

-11-

JEALOUSY

On the ride home, Debra and her Aunt Kay hardly said a word. They entered the house and the first thing Kay said was, "Let's go sit in the living room."

"Why?"

"Because something is clearly going on with you. I'm concerned, and Joey said very clearly, he thinks we should talk about it."

"We should, but I'm not sure what to say."

"I'm sensing that it may have something to do with me—something I did or said. It's okay if you tell me. I care about you and I want to help you. Please talk to me about it."

"Okay. It bothers me that you are so into Joey and that you totally gush over him."

"Why does that bother you?"

"Because I have feelings for him too. Maybe I'm jealous, or just wish I could be you. Maybe you're what he really wants."

"Debra, if I had known of this ahead of time, I wouldn't have flirted with him the way I did. I never had any intention of a long-term relationship, but he seemed like a great guy to have fun with. But now I'm concerned about you."

"Why?"

There was a long pause while Aunt Kay gathered her thoughts.

"Does he know how you feel about him?"

"Yes. I think so."

"How does he feel about you?"

"He told me he loves me."

"Really? Well, in my experience men only say that when they want sex— No, you didn't!"

"I have been with him three times already, but he never told me he loved me until tonight."

"I think before you get too serious with him you should know more about him."

"Like what?"

"Well for one thing, he's older than *me*, at least twice *your* age. Did you know that?"

"Well, he looks a lot younger. So, why should that matter?"

"It matters because he has a lot more experience than you do and seems like a man who would be attractive to other women. He certainly was to me. I'm concerned that he may be taking advantage of you. Maybe he's just in it for the sex. What do you have in common anyway?"

"Well, we both play pool, we both lost a loved one, we're both physically attractive, and we both enjoy our relationship."

"I hope you don't enjoy it too much. Are you using birth control?"

"Condoms."

"Well, please be careful. You don't want to mess up your life by getting pregnant." She did not let on that it was something she knew a lot about.

"I understand. It's something I think about."

"I'd like to make a suggestion."

"Okay."

"You have your NCLEX nursing exam scheduled for Saturday, three weeks from today. It's very important that you focus on that and that you pass it. And, you also need to schedule interviews and find a job. Tell Joey you need to take a break until you complete all of that. If he loves you, he'll understand."

"Can I trust you not to move in on him while I'm on this break," she said jokingly.

"Of course. I promise."

"Okay. I'll text him tomorrow after church."

"Debbie, come here," her aunt said with feeling. "You may never understand how much I care about you. I would never hurt you."

She wondered, *had Aunt Kay ever called her Debbie before? When she was very young maybe?*

They hugged each other tightly.

-12-

THE BREAK

The next day was Sunday. Joey was no longer a church goer, so he slept in, and did little the rest of the morning— made himself brunch, read the paper, called Brian, played pool, paid bills. It was early afternoon when his cell phone rang and he saw a text from Debra:

> *"Joey, Sorry for my mood last night—time of month. Talked with A. Kay. We're good. Must take a break—job interviews, exam in 3 wks—must study. Then license appl. Very busy. Luv u, Deb."*

Her message, left him with an empty feeling. He wondered if she would be too busy to continue their relationship. He had started to have serious feelings for her, and he certainly enjoyed the sex. But on the other hand, he didn't want to mess up her life, to say nothing of his own. He thought about calling her, but decided against it. He sent a short text back:

> *"OK. Good Luck on exam and job hunt. Hope to see U after. Luv U too."*

He needed to take his mind off her, so he donned his leather jacket and helmet and took his bike out for a ride on the nearby trails. It was almost dark when he finally returned.

For the next week and a half, Joey buried himself in his work. He had plenty of experience in his life temporarily compartmentalizing thoughts and feelings that interfered with the task at hand. But then on Wednesday of the second week, while at work, he received a phone call from Doctor Isaac Abraham. Isaac was a colleague, but also a client. Isaac was about to open a new medical clinic and Joey had coordinated the design and purchase of the security system. The installation stage was about to begin.

"Joey, I need to know if we're on schedule. I want to be sure we can open on the first Monday in April."

"Absolutely. The contractors will complete the cabling in another week, and they will install the cameras and security system by March first. Except for training, they will complete all the work on my end by mid-March. You'll have two weeks to move in your furniture and medical apparatus. We can also begin our training during those two weeks."

"That's great. Uh, Joey, there was another reason for my call."

"Oh?"

"Last week, I interviewed a young lady named Debra Johnston. She is looking for a nursing position. Says you referred her."

"I did. What do you think of her?"

"She presented herself well and she gave me two references. One was a doctor in a clinic in Arizona she worked in while a college student. The other was her aunt who lives locally and is a lawyer. But she doesn't have her license yet, and still needs to pass her NCLEX exam. She asked if I would consider hiring her in an administrative position until she had that. I said I would consider that. But I wondered how you knew her and if you could tell me a little more about her."

"I'll tell you what I know," Joey responded, but realized he needed to be careful how he answered that question.

"I've only known her for about six weeks. I know her aunt, Kathy Johnston, who is a reputable lawyer, and is also a member of the Chamber. Anyway, after Debra arrived here from Arizona, the three of us celebrated her twenty-second birthday, and I got to know more about Debra. She struck me as very smart and goal oriented. She told me she was going to be a nurse and had already applied for her license but still needed to take the nursing test and get a job. I offered to help."

"I see. Did she say why she came to New Mexico to start her career?"

"Yes. As I understand it, her father passed away— apparently murdered. Her father was Kathy Johnston's brother. Debra was the one who found his body. The police are investigating his death, and Debra has provided the police with evidence. But according to Debra, the evidence points to her mom's boyfriend, and even to her mom, as being involved. Her mom and dad had separated and her mom did not want Debra to visit him. But she did anyway. That caused tension between Debra and her mom. So, after she got her degree, she decided to move to Albuquerque and live with her aunt until she could afford her own place."

"So, do you think there's a chance that *she* did it? Would I be risking my reputation if I hired her?"

"I don't think you would be taking a risk. She said that the police cleared her. You might get more details from her aunt. I've had several conversations with Debra, and if she had a BS in *engineering* and applied for a job in *my* company, I would hire her."

"Thanks for your input. I trust your judgement, but just to be on the safe side I think I will talk to her aunt. Thanks again."

Once again, he had a desire to call Debra, but refrained from doing so. She planned to take her nursing exam this coming Saturday, and he had promised to give her the space she needed. Just then, his secretary appeared in his doorway.

"Joey, they want you in the conference room."

"Thank you, Jennifer. Be right there."

***

Meanwhile, Debra focused on her future career. She had completed several job interviews with mixed results. None resulted in an offer as a nurse. Typically, they would tell her that they would keep her in mind but to come back after she had her credentials. Two offered her an administrative position. One was not available until April first, about six weeks away. The other was available on Monday, a week. However, she liked the April offer better. It was with Doctor Isaac Abraham and Joey had referred her. He said she could transition to nursing duties as soon as she had her license. But she needed to prepare for the nursing exam, so she deferred a decision until after the exam.

The exam took place on Saturday at the local university campus. It went well, she thought. They allowed her six hours but she only needed four. She assumed she passed, but would not know officially for a few weeks. The Nursing Board would need to review the test results and do a background check to assure there had been no cheating or unworthiness on her part. Then she would receive her credentials. Of course, she told Aunt Kay how she thought she did and about the job offer she hoped to land. That evening they celebrated Debra's success. On Sunday, she received a text message from Joey. She was pleased that he hadn't forgotten and was eager to answer.

Joey: *"How did you do on your exam?"*
Debra: *"Very well, but not official yet. Miss you."*
Joey: *"Are we still on break?"*
Debra: *"How about next Saturday?"*
Joey: *"It's a date."*

Later that week, Debra received an unexpected call from the Yavapai County Sheriff's Department. When they asked for her by name, she had a moment of anxious anticipation. They said they wanted to interview her again regarding the death of her father. She promptly told them they would have to talk to her lawyer, and gave them the number of Aunt Kay's law office.

That evening, Aunt Kay explained what it was all about. The police said they needed Debra to help them provide more evidence before they could go to trial. Aunt Kay scheduled a conference call from her office on Friday. Kathy Johnston was an experienced defense lawyer. She knew that second interviews often meant the police were closing in on a suspect and would try to trip them up and cause them to incriminate themselves. She would make sure that didn't happen to Debra.

-13-

THE GLITCH

Saturday was a beautiful day. The sun was out and temperatures would reach into the fifties. Joey had just finished breakfast, when Debra rang his doorbell. They greeted each other with a hug and a kiss and she followed him to the kitchen. They sat at the table and he offered her coffee and Danish while they talked.

"So, congratulations on doing well on your exam," he told her. "You must be feeling a sense of relief."

"Yes, I am, at least about that, and on the positive side I have two possible job offers. I say possible because I must have my credentials in hand, and that may take another three weeks. I am particularly interested in Doctor Abraham's new East Side Clinic. And thanks for the recommendation. However, like all good things, there may be a glitch that—"

"A glitch?"

"Remember, I told you about my father's murder and that I told the police that I thought my mother's boyfriend Russ may have done it. I think I also said my mother could be involved. And then there's Eddie. They may all have been in on it, and until yesterday, I thought the police still suspected me."

"The glitch?"

"Yes. Yesterday, the Yavapai Sheriff's Department had a conference call with me and my lawyer—Aunt Kay. They want me to come down there and wear a wire and get Eddie to indict his uncle—"

"Okay, I need to catch up. Who is Eddie?"

"Russ is Mom's boyfriend. Eddie is Russ's nephew. Eddie and Russ live in the same house."

"Got it. . . So, are you going to do it?"

"Aunt Kay said she thinks it sounds risky. She said she would let them know by Tuesday."

"So why would Eddie want to talk with you? Do you know him very well?"

"Well, sort of. I don't want to hide this from you. Eddie was my boyfriend, but I broke it off with him more than a year ago. I caught him with my friend Susan and then he got rough with me. However, we're still friends. After my dad died, it took two months before they ruled homicide by poison. Then the police interrogated me and Eddie. In their minds, we were the logical perpetrators. The police believed that Eddie had received fentanyl in the mail, and I certainly had the means to put it into dad's Nutri-Balance capsule. When interrogated, we both told the police that Mom and Uncle Russ were together the week prior to Dad's murder. It was the night after the police said Eddie received the fentanyl. After our interrogations, Eddie and I talked and he let a few things slip out about the role he played and what he observed between Russ and my mom— much more than what he had told the police."

"What do you think his role was?"

"He told me that he unwittingly helped his uncle obtain fentanyl. He told the police that he received a package in the mail addressed to his uncle, never opened it, didn't know what was in it, and gave it to his uncle."

"And what does he know about what Russ and your mother did?"

"He thinks he overheard them talking the night Mom went over to his house. He thinks they were preparing the poison capsule, and he told me that the next morning, he saw evidence."

"He obviously confided in you. Didn't he tell any of this to the police?"

"No, he didn't. He lawyered up. Eddie told me he's scared to death of his uncle. He fears that if he snitches on his uncle, his uncle might try to kill him. Eddie also knows that if he says too much, the sheriff could arrest him on drug charges. It wouldn't be his first one either—another reason I broke up with him."

"I see. Well, I don't know what the sheriff told you about wearing a wire, but it doesn't need to be very risky— depends on how they do it. A few years ago, the police would require you to schedule a meeting with the target— Eddie in this case. The police would then sit in a van a couple of blocks away. You would wear a small microphone and transmitter and the police would listen and record everything. To do this they would either need your consent or have a warrant. However, there is a much better way to do it today. It's less risky and you can do it when and where *you* decide. I would like to demonstrate. Are you willing?"

"I guess. What do I have to do?"

"Give me a few minutes, while I get something I need to show you, and meet me in the living room."

"Okay, I'll be there after I clear the table."

When she returned to the living room, Joey smiled and motioned for her to take a seat on the sofa. As she sat down, he removed a small rectangular shaped black object from his pocket and handed it to her. It looked very much like an oversized USB port flash drive or thumb drive. It was no more than two and a half inches long, three-quarters of an inch wide, and three-eighths of an inch thick.

"What is that?" she asked.

"I'll explain later. Just set it somewhere out of the way—over there on the end table would be fine."

"It's good to see you again Debra. It's been a long time since you left town. How are you getting along with your aunt?"

"Uh . . . Really well . . . Eddie." She caught on and played along. "And you? How are you and your Uncle Russ doing?"

They continued to play-act for a few more minutes before Joey suggested that they could stop.

"Now pick up the device and come with me," he said.

She picked up the small black device, and followed him down the stairs, past the pool table to a small room behind the stairs. She watched closely as Joey punched a number into the reader next to the door. As they entered, he flicked a light switch, and shut the door behind them. Inside, Debra noticed that the room was strangely quiet—no sound from outside. She followed Joey passed file cabinets and storage boxes to a back corner. There, a computer and other electronic devices sat upon a small table.

"What is all this?" she asked.

"This is my security system," he replied. "Now, please hand me the device," he said. "This device is a professional quality voice-activated digital voice recorder—state of the art. We should have a recording of everything we said up to now."

Joey took possession of the device and stopped the recording by turning a small loop at one end of the device. He removed a cap from the other end of the device, and plugged the device into his computer. He then accessed a file on the computer screen, and entered a code. The conversation they had upstairs began to play with great clarity on speakers that hung on the wall behind the computer table.

"I can save it onto another thumb drive if I choose, or resend it to an E-mail address, but in this case, we will just delete it. Here. Let me show you how it works. It's very simple. The loop on the end is a switch. Move it that way to continuously record or the other way to voice activate. In the center is off. All the other controls are inside and preset. To recharge, put it in the off position and stick it into a USB port. And if you had a laptop with you," he continued, "you could send it to me or to any other appropriate E-mail address."

"So bottom line, I could record a conversation I have with Eddie or my mom without their knowledge and send it to your computer—"

"Or to the police," he said, finishing her sentence.

"Wow, I'm impressed!" she said. "But I have a question. Are you sure it's legal if I record someone without their knowledge? Can the police use it in court?"

"I'm quite certain it's legal in Arizona and in New Mexico. Your aunt's a criminal lawyer and can verify that. Debra, if you decide to go to Arizona, I'd like you to take this device with you," he said and handed it to her. "It's not a toy. Only use it if you need to and don't lose it."

"Okay, thanks," she said and put it into her pocket. "Joey, your process sounds less risky than wearing a wire. The sheriff wasn't very specific as to how they would do it, so there may be some risk and this may be better. But, I'm also not sure how good of an actress I may need to be to get Eddie to say what the sheriff wants to hear. I don't want to give myself away and have him get rough with me."

"That begs the question. When he asks what made you decide to come back, what do you tell him?"

"Well, I don't need to lie. I'm somewhat homesick and I also want to visit my dad's gravesite. They had not engraved and installed his headstone until after I left in January. And regardless of what she may have done, I want to see my mom. I want to maintain a relationship with her. I mean after all she is my mom. And I miss my friends, Susan especially, and even Eddie. And, if I'm going to go back to Cornville this would be a good time to do it. I just passed my nursing exam and I don't start a full-time job until a month from now."

"Sounds like you've got it covered."

"Do you think I should do it?"

Joey turned toward her and put his hands on her shoulders. "Debra, talk to Aunt Kay, but the decision is yours to make; not mine; not your aunts. You're smart and you know yourself better than anyone else does. Don't underestimate your capabilities. Consider the possible outcomes of whichever decision you make. Evaluate possible benefits and downsides, and their likelihoods. Make the best decision you can with the information you have, and go for it. Regardless of how it turns out, own it and know you did the best you could. And, also know that I will support you one hundred percent, and I think your aunt will as well."

She seemed lost in thought. "You know," he added. "Sometimes it helps to temporarily put it aside and come back to it later."

She looked at him and smiled. "You're right. It's a nice day today. What should we do?"

"How about a motorcycle ride? I know a scenic place up in the hills where we can have a picnic lunch. We can stop at Pedro's and get some take-out to bring with us."

"Sounds good."

-14-

HOLDING TIGHT

Joey opened the garage door and introduced Debra to his bike, a Hawk 250 cc, 5-speed manual shift, electric kick start, street legal, big-wheeled dirt bike.

"Did you say this will be your first time on a bike?"

"I did. I'm a little nervous."

"Don't be. You're going to enjoy it."

He grabbed two jackets from a nearby hook and handed one to her.

"Isn't it too warm for this?" she asked

"Once we're on the road you'll be grateful to have it. Believe me."

He paused then looked at her again. "I need you to also put on this knapsack."

She gave him a look, as he continued. "It's the only way we have to carry our lunch."

"Why can't . . . oh I get it," she said realizing why the alternative wouldn't work as well.

Joey walked the bike out to the driveway. "Now, one more thing. I'd like you to please put on that helmet," he said pointing to the rear of the bike.

After locking up the garage and the house, he mounted the bike.

"Climb aboard and keep your arms around my waist at all times," he instructed.

She situated herself as instructed. Her arms were around his waist and her chest was up against his back. He kick-started the engine and they were off.

They picked up two chicken rice bowls and two ginger ales at Pedro's and then went east to the hills and trails. As they hit the first winding dirt trail the ride became bumpy.

"Hold on tight!" he yelled.

The trail was narrow with short rises and depressions, and gullies often lined the sides. Joey could often feel Debra's arms tighten around his waist only to relax a moment later, and then suddenly tighten again. He also could hear strange sounds from her mouth alternating between blood curdling screams and hysterical laughter. After a while they made it near the top of a hill where they would picnic. As soon as they dismounted, and removed their helmets, he turned to her and asked,

"Are you okay?"

"More than okay. I loved it! It was better than any amusement park rides I've ever been on."

He grinned. "For a moment there, I wasn't sure."

They took a short walk up to the peak where they could see for miles. They could see the city back to the southwest and more hills to the north. They took photos, including selfies, and then they enjoyed lunch, and talked, mostly about nothing important.

***

They were back in the house by mid-afternoon. Debra used the bathroom to wash up and Joey followed. She was in the living room, sitting in the easy chair, when he returned.

"So, what do you think? You up for a game of eight-ball?" he asked.

"Yes, but I want to talk with you about something first."

"Sure. What would you like to talk about?"

"Our relationship."

He could tell from her expression and tone that she was serious.

"Oh . . . is there a problem?" he asked and took a seat on the edge of the sofa.

She observed a worried look on his face.

"No," she chuckled. "I'm not breaking up with you. I want to talk to you about the conversation I had with Aunt Kay after the dinner at El Palacio. If you remember, I was acting childish and jealous of Aunt Kay, and before you left, you said that she and I should talk."

"Of course. You told me you talked and everything was okay."

"Well, it's okay, but I want you to know what we said. I told her that I was jealous of her overtures toward you because I had feelings for you. She said that had she known, she wouldn't have been so flirtatious with you. But then, she suggested that I focus on my career goals and not rush into a relationship. That advice led to our three-week break—and by the way, I appreciated you understanding. Then, she suggested that I needed to know more about you, and that maybe you were only interested in me for the sex. I told her that just before we left El Palacio, you had told me that you loved me—although I'm not sure you meant it the way I heard it. She told me that sometimes men will say that to get sex. But then I told her that I already had sex with you before you said it. She repeated her advice that I get to know you better and that I not rush into anything."

He could tell by the look on her face that she wanted him to respond at that point.

"I remember telling you that I loved you and not your aunt. It wasn't something that I had planned to say ahead of time, but I've had three weeks to think about it, and I can assure you that I really do love you."

Her eyes seemed to get misty and turn away. He tried to understand her response.

"Debra? Perhaps you're not sure if you feel the same way about me?"

She instantly looked up, arose from her chair and deposited herself on top of his lap. "I'm more than sure," she told him. She put her arms around his neck and kissed him hard on the mouth. "But this is all new to me, and a little scary."

"We'll do it together, one step at a time. Okay?"

"Okay, but I still want to know more about you."

"I know, and you will, but I need for you to be patient with me on that. Debra, I would like to ask you something." She lifted her head, and looked at him. "Can you spend the night?"

"Can I beat you at pool?" she responded.

-15-

SOMETHING NEW

She beat him at eight-ball, two games out of three. They made a chef salad for dinner. After dinner, she called her aunt to let her know she would be staying overnight. Joey could overhear some slight discord before he heard Debra promise to be home in time for them to go to church. When she finished her call, Joey asked her about that.

"Debra, I don't want you to give up church because of me."

"Kay said I should ask you if you wanted to come. Do you?"

"Well, I must be honest with you about that. My parents brought me up Catholic, but I gave up on the Church many years ago. Too hypocritical in my opinion. But it sounds like your aunt wants you to go with her. It's probably important to her."

"Yeah, but I don't understand that. She goes to a Catholic church and she's very dutiful about it. But growing up, I attended a Protestant church in Cornville with Mom and Dad. How did Dad's sister become a devout Catholic?"

"Hmm, good question. Maybe you should ask her that sometime. In the meantime, if we aren't going to have a lot of time together in the morning, maybe we should retire early. What do you think?"

"Great idea."

"I'd like to suggest we go upstairs to the master bedroom."

"Okay," she said with some trepidation. She had not yet been in the master bedroom and she knew that this was the room he had shared with Brandy.

She followed him up the stairs to a landing at the top. "That door straight ahead goes into the adjoining bathroom," he said. "And that door to the right goes out to a bank of solar collectors. The bedroom is this way," he said and opened a door to their immediate left.

Debra stepped into the room and looked around. A ceiling fan circulated the air. Along the wall to the immediate right, she noticed the door to the adjoining bath and then a clothing closet with sliding doors. On the far end of the room to the right she noticed the picture window facing the mountains. "Wow this is really nice!" she said. His and her dressers stood on the walls on either side of the window. At the other end of the room to the left of the doorway, a king-sized bed projected from the wall flanked by two small windows. Centered on the wall above the head of the bed she noticed a large framed picture of a volcano. Interesting she thought.

The room was clean and without clutter. A colorful spread covered the bed and the two king-sized sleeping pillows. Decorative throw pillows added an inviting touch. Everything seemed too neat—not exactly what she would have expected. She wondered if Joey had even been using this room. Then she wondered if Joey would feel uncomfortable about sleeping here with her—or perhaps she would. After all, this had been Joey and Brandy's marital suite for three years. No need to dance around this. She came right out and asked him.

"Joey, are you sure you're going to be okay with sleeping with me here?"

"Yes, and I want you to be also. Look, I know what you're saying. It's like you miss your dad, but you will always remember him and you will always love him. Likewise, I will always remember Brandy and I will always love her. But it's been several months now for both of us. I think we need to move on."

"Are her things still here?"

"No. Before the holidays, I removed her things. I gave some of it to her son, Brian, and his wife. A couple of things I gave to Peter, Brandy's birth father—things that he or her mother had given her. I kept a few things, and everything else—mostly clothes—I gave to charity."

"I see."

"Debra, are *you* okay with this? If not, we can go down stairs."

"I'll make the effort. Just promise you won't call out her name while you're making love to me." She said jokingly.

"Only if you promise me that you won't call out *Dan*," he said throwing it right back at her."

"Touché."

She spent the night, and for the first time they made love in the master bedroom.

The next morning, they were up early. Joey was first in the bathroom and then went downstairs to prepare breakfast. After her turn in the bathroom, she went over to the picture above the bed to take a closer look. She found it interesting. Most pictures of volcanos she had seen displayed the violence of eruption and the flow of hot lava. This one seemed peaceful. Where the crater would normally hold red molten lava, this one held blue water.

She dressed and went downstairs to join Joey in the kitchen. It smelled delicious. He had prepared a breakfast of fresh fruit, ham and cheese omelets, English muffins, and brewed coffee. During breakfast, she asked him about the picture that hung over the bed.

He thought for a moment before answering. "It's a photograph of the Poás volcano in Costa Rica."

"Did you take the picture?"

"No. Ed, a family friend of Brandy and myself, took the photo many years ago. Then he mounted and framed it. Ed gave it to us as a wedding present. It's symbolic of life. Life can be so serene and peaceful, like in the picture. But then it can erupt unexpectantly and cause vast amount of havoc and destruction."

"Has it ever erupted?"

"It has. On several occasions."

"Were you and Brandy ever there?"

He paused. He knew that he was about to reveal details about his past that could get into the wrong hands. But he needed to trust her, so he answered truthfully.

"Yes. I was there with Ed when he took the photo. I also went there with my father and stepmom when I was a boy. I believe Brandy went there with her son before we were married. Interestingly, we were never there together."

His answer raised more questions in Debra's mind. She had noticed a date on the picture indicating that Ed took the photo in 2002. She wondered if Ed was a family friend of Joey's family long before he knew Brandy? But she decided not to press him. After all, it had been a perfect weekend and he had gone out of his way to please her.

Before she left to meet Kay for church, Debra promised to let him know what she was going to do about the sheriff's request and to keep him in the loop.

On Wednesday evening, she informed him that she and Aunt Kay would fly to Flagstaff early the following Sunday morning, the first Sunday in March. They would rent a car and drive to Cottonwood, where they would stay at the Pioneer Inn, meet with the sheriff on Monday, and meet with Eddie on Tuesday. She E-mailed him the itinerary. In the E-mail she added, "I'll have the voice recorder with me—just in case."

-16-

WELCOME BACK

Debra and Aunt Kay landed at Pulliam Airport in Flagstaff just before noon. They picked up their mid-sized sedan and began the one-hour drive to the Pioneer Inn in Cottonwood. They used Interstate 17 for most of the way but did enjoy a scenic route from the Interstate to Cottonwood via Cornville. They stopped at a fast-food restaurant for a quick lunch on the eastern edge of the town. As they continued through Cornville, they passed the road that led to the Johnston family estate. Then they passed another road that led to the cemetery and grave sites for Debra's dad and the Johnston family. Just to the west of Cornville, they passed an Italian restaurant. Debra pointed it out. She said it didn't look like much but she had been there and the food was excellent. "Perhaps we could come back later for dinner," Aunt Kay suggested. After a stretch of scenic but winding road to the west of Cornville they came to State Route 89-A. Cottonwood and the Pioneer Inn were only two miles more.

Cell phone service was acceptable. So, the first thing Debra did after they checked in was to leave an arrival message for Joey. She then called Eddie to reaffirm their intended meeting Tuesday evening. Then she called Susan. Although it was upsetting at the time, she had forgiven Susan for her affair with Eddie. Susan was her best friend in high school. They were on the softball team together, and both were good students. Susan had taken the time to drive Debra to the airport in January despite the bad weather. They planned to see each other on Monday at noon for lunch.

Debra also called her mom and asked if she could come by and visit. Her mom had never acted cruelly towards her. The main issue she had with her mom was how her mom had treated her dad. Besides, if she didn't visit with her mom, people would wonder why she came back. So, she called, but got a stern rebuff when she mentioned that Aunt Kay was with her. Debra explained that, due to her age, the rental agency would not allow her to drive the car without Aunt Kay, but suggested that perhaps her mom could come pick her up Tuesday for lunch and they could talk. Her mom agreed.

It was now half past three in the afternoon. "What should we do now?" Debra asked.

"It's still warm out—about 55 degrees and sunny. I thought perhaps we should go visit Dan's grave. And then after that we could have dinner at that Italian restaurant we passed on this side of Cornville."

"Sounds like a great idea. Let's do it."

They drove to the cemetery in Cornville. Dan's entire family had been buried there, including his mother, his father, and his younger brother Steven. Steven had died at the age of eighteen from a job site mishap. As Debra and Aunt Kay walked to the family plot it was apparent that no one had recently been there. Weeds had grown around the gravestones including Dan's new headstone. Aunt Kay expressed her displeasure. Debra tried to console her. "Aunt Kay, I'm sorry."

Debra pulled up as many weeds as she could around Dan's marker. "Aunt Kay, Dan's headstone turned out perfect. Don't you think?" she asked.

Aunt Kay looked at her. "Yes, I do," she said weakly and forced a smile.

"Aunt Kay, you may not have known this but Dan was the one who maintained the plot. He came here every other weekend to weed, plant flowers, and do whatever else was needed. I came here four months ago and did the same, but it looks like the flowers we planted by Dan's grave didn't make it through the winter. There's no one else to do this now. Mom refuses to come. I think she hated Dan and she was not close to any of the other Johnstons that are here. Perhaps we could find time tomorrow to come back here and pull weeds. We could stop at the nursery on the way and pick up some flowers to plant."

"Yes Debra, that's a good idea. We should do that. But then what?"

"We'll find someone to do it on a regular basis."

After spending several minutes at Dan's gravestone, Aunt Kay went over to Steven's grave. When Debra looked over there, she sensed that Aunt Kay was crying. Debra walked over, gently put her hand on her aunt's shoulder and asked, "Are you okay?"

"I'm fine. The three of us were very close. I was especially close to Steven. He died so unexpectedly at such a young age." Debra noticed the date of death on the tombstone was only three months after her own birthday.

Then they went to the tombstone of Dan and Steven's mother, and Debra saw that Dan's mother had died only a year after Steven. "It all happened in such a short time," Aunt Kay said. "Grandpa Johnston had passed away two years before and Grandma Johnston was ailing. Dan and your mom came back to help. We all lived in the family house and we all enjoyed taking care of you until I moved to New Mexico and then it was only Dan and your mom." Debra had questions, but considering Aunt Kay's display of emotions, decided that this was not the time.

Dinner was next. An elderly Italian couple operated the restaurant and the food was genuine Italian cuisine. It was quite to their liking. They each enjoyed a glass of chianti with their meal—but only one. It was only half-past seven when they left, but the sun had set and it was now dark, and the temperature had dropped. The forecast was for the temperature to go below freezing before morning. As soon as they got into the car, they put on the jackets that Aunt Kay had suggested they carry with them.

The plan was to drive back to the Pioneer Inn and get a good night's sleep before meeting with the sheriff in the morning. As they headed west toward Cottonwood, the road began a long ascent over a mountain. The darkness of night and the lack of street lighting limited their visibility. The scenic views from earlier in the day were now gone. To be safe, Aunt Kay made sure she did not exceed the speed limit. They had just passed the crest and were beginning their descent when they noticed another vehicle come up from behind at a rapid pace. Aunt Kay peered into the rearview mirror, but the other vehicle's high beams made recognition impossible. Debra noticed it as well. "Perhaps he wants to pass you," she suggested. Aunt Kay slowed, hoping the unexpected intruder would pass once they were beyond the upcoming curve, but that's not what happened. The other vehicle stayed right on her tail almost bumper to bumper. Then unexpectedly she felt a jolt. Rather than pass her, it had bumped her rear. Aunt Kay accelerated, but as she exited another curve and continued down the hill, the other vehicle remained on her tail. They could hear the loud exhaust of their pursuer as it accelerated and then seemed to be about to pass as they came to a straight section of road. But instead, it rammed the left side of her rear bumper and continued to push, causing her car to veer sharply to the right. Her right front wheel went off the pavement first, and as it did, the car spun 180 degrees. They were now going backwards and sideways at the same time. Debra grabbed for the door with her right arm before they smashed sideways into an embankment. They slid backwards along the embankment for another moment causing a loud screeching sound as car metal engaged stone. Debra felt pain in her arm as the impact forced her to let go of the door. Her lap belt cut into her waist while her upper body snapped sideways, unprotected by the shoulder belt. Then everything went deadly still and quiet. When Debra regained her composure, the first thing she did was to call out to Aunt Kay. She got no response. "**Aunt Kay, Aunt Kay,**" she screamed. The engine had died but the headlights were still on. She switched on the interior light, found her cell phone and dialed 911. Fortunately, the call went through.

Debra rode with Aunt Kay in the ambulance to the same local hospital where she had worked less than a year ago. While in transport, Aunt Kay regained consciousness. That was a good sign, but Debra knew that the bruising on the left side of her head meant that she would need extensive testing. She would be lucky if all she had was a concussion. By the time they reached the emergency room, Debra was beginning to feel more pain in her own body as well.

***

When they arrived at the hospital, Debra and Aunt Kay were separated. A medic told Debra they would see each other later. A registered nurse examined Debra. Her neck hurt when she turned her head. An x-ray showed no damage to her spine, but the nurse offered a neck brace for her sprained neck, which Debra accepted. Her right shoulder hurt when she raised her arm, but x-rays showed it was not dislocated. The nurse offered a sling, but she declined. And, her midriff had bruises on the left side but a scan revealed no internal injury. After a short discussion, a doctor agreed to release her. He wrote her a prescription for pain medication if she needed it, but also suggested Tylenol. Upon release, Debra immediately asked to see Aunt Kay. They told her she must wait until they completed more tests, but they would let her know as soon as they knew something. She went to a waiting room where she could make cell phone calls. She called Joey.

He picked up on the third ring, and saw that the caller ID belonged to Debra. "Debra, what's going on?"

"Joey, Joey, I'm in the hospital. I'm okay, but Aunt Kay is hurt badly and I'm waiting for the doctor to come back out." The emotion in her voice was apparent.

"Oh my God. What happened?"

"We were going back to our hotel from dinner, and someone forced us off the road. Aunt Kay has a head injury, and who knows what else. She may be here awhile. I'm upset. I just needed to talk to you."

"Oh Debra. I'm so sorry. I don't want you to be upset. How are you physically? Did they check you out?"

"Yes, I have a sprained neck from whiplash, my right shoulder and wrist hurts, and my waist is black and blue from the lap belt. They said I was free to go, but I need to stay here until I know how Aunt Kay is."

"What hospital are you at?"

"The Verde Valley Medical Center in Cottonwood."

"Did you say someone forced you off the road? Are you able to file a police report?"

"Not yet. Seems they only work in the daytime. We were supposed to meet with the sheriff in the morning. Don't think we can do that now. And I have no transportation anyway."

"Debra, I want to be there to help you. I'm going to fly down there in the morning. Tell me your hotel room number."

"205 . . . no, no," she whimpered. "I wasn't expecting that." She started crying.

"Debra, I love you. Hang in there. I'll be there."

Several minutes later the doctor came out to the waiting room.

"Are you Ms. Johnston's daughter?" he asked.

"No. I'm her niece. Why did you think I was her daughter?"

"When she was still semi-conscious, she kept asking for her daughter. Does she have a daughter? Was someone else in the car?"

"No . . . and no," Debra answered, still puzzled.

"Perhaps she was just delirious. She has a broken left wrist. She's lucky she was wearing a heavy jacket. A shard of glass cut right through it but only nicked her wrist. She also has a fractured collar bone, and a mild concussion, and she's in pain. We had to give her something for that. She is conscious now and as soon as we get her a room you may see her. However, she will need to be here overnight and possibly another day. My nurse, Sally Smith, tells me you used to work here and she knows you. She said she will come and talk to you."

"Thank you."

Sally Smith was several years older than Debra. The two of them got along well. Sally had been somewhat of a mentor when Debra was here working part-time. Sally gave her more information about Aunt Kay's condition. She would need to be here until they could be sure she had no brain swelling or bleeding. Then she would need rest. She asked where they were staying and told her how to get a cab ride to and from the hospital. "I'd take you myself if you're still here, but I don't get off until midnight," she said. An orderly notified them that they were moving Aunt Kay to a permanent room. Debra followed the gurney down the corridor, into a private room.

As soon as the orderlies left, Debra went to Aunt Kay's side, held her hand, and they talked. Aunt Kay seemed tired but alert.

"I'm so sorry Debra."

"No need to apologize. They told me I was okay. They said you would be okay as well—it would just take a little longer."

"Debra, I need you to reschedule that meeting in the morning. I should be at the meeting."

"I know, but trust me, if you can't be there, I can handle it. I still want to go through with the plan."

"As your lawyer, my concern is that something may be said that would put you at risk or implicate you in the crime."

"I'll call them in the morning. Maybe, if you're up to it, they could do it here in the hospital."

Aunt Kay released her hand. "Debra, you should get back to the hotel and get some sleep."

"Okay. I'll see you in the morning and let you know what is happening."

Debra followed Sally's instructions and arranged for a cab. She was back at the Pioneer Inn before midnight.

-17-

AFTERMATH

Her alarm sounded earlier the next morning than she would have liked. As she twisted her body and reached for the alarm with her right hand the pain from her injuries quickly returned. The pain had kept her awake until she took one of the pills the nurse had given her. She could have used another hour or two in bed, but she had work to do. She got herself together, put her neck brace on, and went to the lobby to satisfy her hunger at the free breakfast bar. A Danish, an orange juice, and two Tylenols were enough. Once back in her room, she called the City of Cottonwood Police Department and asked to speak to Detective Logan, the investigator assigned to her case. He was not there yet. She left a message that she needed to reschedule their 9:00 a.m. meeting—to please call.

The City of Cottonwood only had one active detective at that time and had called upon the County Sheriff's Department for help. A representative from the Sheriff's Department had set up the 9:00 a.m. meeting and was also supposed to attend. While waiting for a call back, Debra called the hospital and talked with Aunt Kay. Aunt Kay told her a local patrol officer had talked with her about the accident and filed a report, but she still couldn't remember everything that happened and suggested he talk to her as well. At 8:50 a.m., Debra received a call from a Lieutenant Armstrong, with the County Sheriff's Department. Apparently, he had driven all the way up from his office in Prescott for the meeting. He wanted to know what happened. She told him everything she could over the phone.

"Are we still scheduled to do the surveillance tomorrow?" he asked.

"Yes, but my aunt wanted us to meet beforehand. She is acting as my lawyer. We were wondering if we could have the meeting at the hospital."

"Perhaps she is well enough that we could do that. Let me call and find out. I'll get back to you."

Armstrong arranged a meeting in the hospital for early that afternoon, for the three of them plus Detective Logan. Armstrong scheduled the meeting at the hospital for 1:00 p.m. Debra had a lunch date with Susan, so Debra called Susan to update her.

She told Susan about the accident and that they would only have about forty minutes together for lunch. Susan expressed concern about Debra's condition as well as Kay's condition. She offered to cancel but Debra insisted she come anyway, even if the visit was short. Susan agreed.

Susan arrived at the Pioneer Inn around noon. She surprised Debra by bringing sandwiches to share for lunch. The two of them did the best they could to catch up in the short time they had available. During their conversation, Susan mentioned that Eddie had talked to her earlier and they talked about the accident. She also said that she didn't like the idea of Eddie having dinner with her tomorrow. She said that she and Eddie were still dating and that they were getting serious. Debra assured her that she had nothing to worry about. She and Eddie were just old friends, and besides she had a regular boyfriend of her own.

Shortly thereafter, Detective Logan picked Debra up and drove her to the hospital. At the meeting, they all agreed upon the terms of the surveillance of Eddie. The detectives would begin to follow him tomorrow when he left work around 4:30 p.m. Eddie had already agreed to meet Debra at 5:00 p.m. at the Pioneer Inn. They then planned to go to a nearby diner for supper and conversation. The detectives gave her a small listening device, and explained how to conceal it on her person. "This device will transmit your conversation with Eddie to us. We will be in a nearby vehicle listening and recording," Detective Logan told her. The device was larger and bulkier than the one she had received from Joey, and she wondered if it would be easy to conceal it as instructed.

"Why would you need to be there and listen?" she asked, as she tucked the device into her purse alongside the recorder previously given to her by Joey.

"Just in case anything should go wrong, we want to be there to protect you," Armstrong responded.

After the meeting at the hospital, Detective Logan drove her back to the Inn.

As fate would have it, they didn't have to wait until the next day for things to go wrong.

-18-

VISIT WITH EDDIE

Back at the inn, Debra removed her cardigan and her shoes, collapsed on the bed and fell asleep. A short time later, she was awakened by someone knocking on the door. A glance at her watch told her it was 4:30 p.m. Then she remembered. Last night, Joey had told her he would fly there as soon as he could. She was excited as she opened the door to let him in.

"Jo—" Her jaw dropped. "Eddie, what are you doing here? I thought we were on for tomorrow."

"We were, but I found out about your accident. It was all over the local news this morning. You seem disappointed that it's me."

"To be honest, I *was* expecting someone else but I had fallen asleep—"

"May I come in? Or would you rather I leave?"

His tone was sincere, not sarcastic, and he had that puppy dog look. She couldn't resist.

"Uhm . . . sure. Come in. Make yourself comfortable. How did you know my room number?"

"I asked. It's a small town. They know me here."

"Ah, well . . . please give me a moment while I get myself together and then we can talk."

She grabbed her purse, her cardigan, and her shoes and headed into the bathroom. After she used the toilet, washed, and combed the knots out of her hair, she adjusted her neck brace, donned the cardigan, and transferred Joey's recorder from her purse to the pocket of the cardigan. She set the switch to voice-activate. When she returned to the main room, Eddie had already removed his coat and was sitting in the easy-chair across from the bed. Debra got back onto her bed and propped herself up against two pillows.

"Deb, it looks like you're hurt. You're wearing a neck brace. Are you okay?"

"I'll be okay. I have a strained neck and an injured shoulder and waist. No broken bones though. My Aunt Kay is a little worse off. She has a head injury and a broken collar bone. She's still in the hospital. How about you Eddie? You look good."

"I'm doing good and staying out of trouble. Trying to get my life back on track."

"That's good to hear Eddie."

"I thought you would be staying with your mom. Why here?" he asked.

"She still has a problem with me. Doesn't want me stirring up trouble, and still blames me for holding up her insurance payment for my dad's policy. I called her yesterday before the accident and offered to take her to dinner, but she told me she didn't want to see Aunt Kay."

"Why?"

"Aunt Kay and my dad were close, and Aunt Kay was angry with Mom when she kicked him out of the house. I thought I told you all this."

"Yeah, you did. Sorry."

"Speaking of my mom, is she still seeing your Uncle Russ?"

"Not so much since January. I think they had a falling out."

"Why?"

"The police had interviewed all of us. The questions they asked me led me to think the police suspected the two of them had conspired to commit the murder."

"Yes, that makes sense. After they cleared me, the two of them were the prime suspects."

He continued. "In early January, I overheard a phone call they had with each other. You and your mother always called on the landline because the cell phone reception between here and Cornville was never that good. Anyway, I have a land line extension phone in my room. The caller ID said it was your mother. I was curious, so I put it on mute and listened in. The conversation was not very lovey-dovey. She accused him of allowing the authorities to trace the drug order back to our house, and he accused her of falsely telling him the death would look like a heart attack. She told him that the police thought he did it, and she thought it would be better if they didn't see each other again until things blew over. He responded by saying he thought she loved him and would stand by him. 'Not if I end up in jail,' she had said."

"I bet that hurt."

"It did. A couple of days later, Uncle Russ seemed to be in a bad mood. I casually mentioned to him that I hadn't seen your mother over here lately. He told me they had a falling out. I asked him if it had something to so with Mr. Johnston's murder. He said that it did. 'You seem upset by it,' I said. He told me that after everything he had done for her, she didn't want to see him anymore. Yes, he was upset."

"Do you think when he said, 'after everything he had done for her' he was talking about the murder of my dad?"

"I do. I know you don't want to hear it but I think that your mother instigated the whole thing."

"Eddie, there are still people that think I killed him. I had the means and some people think that my motivation was that I resented his sexual advances toward me. I also received a small amount of money from a bank account he had. One of the reasons I'm here is because I need to clear my name. I want to be a registered nurse and my application is under review. If they don't charge someone else, I may have to live with the stigma of possibly poisoning someone. I could use your help."

"What can I do?" he said and shrugged his shoulders.

"The reason no one has been charged is because the police can't prove where the poison came from and who used it. It would really help if you told the police what you know."

"Didn't we already have this conversation? They asked me if I knew you, and what I knew about Uncle Russ and so on. But when they started talking about drugs, I clammed up."

"Didn't you tell me that Russ bought fentanyl online and had it mailed to your house? And didn't you tell me that you were home when Russ and my mom met in the den and most likely prepared the poisoned capsule?"

"Yes, I did."

"Wasn't that the Wednesday before my dad died?"

"Yes, it was."

Debra remembered that shortly after supper, her mother had told her she was going to Russ's house. "Don't wait up" she had said. "I plan to spend the night." It was unusual for her to spend the night at Russ's on a weeknight and her mom already had a bag packed. Debra was curious, so when she had the chance, she peeked in. In addition to clothes and toiletries she also saw a bottle of Nutri-Balance, latex gloves, surgical masks, and a small bottle of an unknown substance. But before she could search any further her mom had come back into the room. *What were they up to?* she had wondered. So, after her mom left for Russ's house, she got onto her mom's desktop computer and read her mom's downloaded E-mail. She came across a plain text E-mail from Russ. "I have the F tabs. Please come for the night and bring your stuff." Her mother had responded "I will be there." Debra remembered that the next day she had asked her mom about the visit and her mom had been evasive. Debra had told all of this to the police and was sure that they would see the E-mail exchange and other E-mails as part of their investigation. But now she needed to get Eddie to say what he knew.

"Eddie, what did they do that night? What did you see?"

"Your mother arrived around nine. She had a medium sized bag with her. The two of them retired to the den and shut the door. I had to work an early shift on Thursday so I went up to my room."

"What about the next morning? Didn't you tell me you went into the den before they got up and found evidence of what they had done? Isn't that what you told me?"

"Yes, but I also told you that Uncle Russ threatened to kill me if I mentioned anything I knew to the police."

"I'm not the police. I need to know what my mother did. I want to know what you saw and heard."

"Okay. I got up early that morning. Your mother and Uncle Russ were still upstairs asleep. I was curious so I entered the den. I saw a small ash tray with discarded damaged capsules. Some of the capsules were empty and the contents were in the ash tray. I also saw a bottle of Nutri-Balance on top of the desk, and a mortar and pestle. The mortar was moist and half filled with what looked like rice."

"It's a way to clean it. Did you find any leftover fentanyl?"

"It was also on Russ's desk. They come in packs of ten. The package said 1000 mcg. Six tablets remained. They must have ground up the other four."

"Yeah, if Dad absorbed all of it, four would have been more than a lethal amount. Anything else?"

"I saw a small bottle of some drug. I'm not sure, what it was."

"Could it have been Nembutal?"

"No . . . I'm not sure."

"How about Ketamine?"

"Maybe. I really don't remember. But I don't understand. If four fentanyl tablets were more than lethal, why would they need anything else?"

"Well, whatever it was, it would make sense. Ingested fentanyl would take time to enter Dad's system. They may have added another drug to render him unconscious so that he couldn't react before the fentanyl took effect. Or, they may have added a drug that increased the amount of fentanyl that his body absorbed."

"Deb, you really know about this stuff, don't you?"

"Drugs were the subject of one of the courses I took while earning my nursing degree. I got an A plus."

"I wouldn't have guessed anything less," he said.

"Eddie, what else did you see in the den?"

"I also saw a small plastic container."

"What did it look like?"

"Like a small pill bottle. It was orange but transparent. It had a white snap-cap on top. And now that I think about it, one Nutri-Balance capsule was inside. Do you think that was the poison pill?"

"Hmm . . . I do, because later that day, I found an empty pill bottle that looked just like that. I went over to Dad's apartment to study. When I arrived, the door was open and I called out to find out who was there. It was Russ. 'Maintenance,' he replied. I think I startled him. He met me at the door very quickly. Of course, he had an excuse as to why he was there. He said he was investigating a water leak that was going into an apartment below. We talked for a few minutes and then he left. I told all of that to the police. But later I found an orange bottle on the kitchen floor just like what you described. It was hiding under a chair. It looked like something useful, so I picked it up and set it on the back of the counter top, out of the way. I didn't think any more about it until after Dad died. But then I remembered the bottle and wondered if it could have been the bottle that Russ carried the pill in. Perhaps he dropped it when I unexpectedly entered the apartment. I knew it had my fingerprints on it, but I thought that my mom's and Russ's prints might also be on it. The bottle could have come from the pharmacy where Mom works. I also thought there was a chance that trace evidence of fentanyl could have been in the bottle. I told the police about it and they took it into evidence."

"Did the police learn anything from the bottle?"

"I don't know Eddie. I was a suspect. They didn't tell me anything. Did you find anything else in the den?"

"Yes. I looked in the wastebasket in the den. The mailing envelope for the drugs was in there."

"Did you find anything else in the wastebasket?"

"Yeah . . . I did. Two discarded face masks and latex gloves."

"Eddie let me ask you something. After you observed all these items didn't that concern you?"

"Not at the time. I wish I had. Maybe I could have stopped it, but at the time I just didn't piece it together. I had no idea they were planning to kill your dad and I feel bad about that. Deb, I'm not smart like you. I remember things but I don't know how to analyze them and reach conclusions like you. I'm sorry. I really am. Please, forgive me."

She knew him well enough to know he was sincere.

"I forgive you Eddie, but it seems to me my mom and your uncle are guilty as hell."

"I don't disagree, but what should we do about it? We're talking about *my* uncle and *your* mother."

"Eddie, we're also talking about my dad. He's dead! I need you to do the right thing and tell all of this to the police. If my mom and your uncle did this, we need to hold them accountable. If you try to keep this a secret, it will end up destroying you psychologically. Believe me!"

"If I do this, do you think we could ever be together again?"

"Eddie, do you remember why we broke up?"

"I remember that Uncle Russ told me you had sex with your father, and when I asked you if that was why you were breaking up with me, you said yes it was."

"Eddie, I was being sarcastic. I saw you with my friend Susan. And when I asked you about it, you demanded sex and got rough with me. Eddie, I can't promise you that we will be together again," she said in a gentle tone. "But I will respect you, and be grateful, and you will feel good about yourself."

"What if the police implicate me as well? I already have a minor drug offense."

"Why would they implicate you? Your uncle ordered the fentanyl. Not your fault."

There was a pause. "I didn't tell you everything."

"Oh?"

"Uncle Russ doesn't know diddlysquat about ordering things on the Internet. He came to me and said he had a friend who had cancer. Said his friend needed fentanyl tablets to manage the pain. He wanted the strongest tabs possible for him, and he asked me to help him order it—"

She stopped him before he could incriminate himself.

"Eddie, you don't need to tell me how you helped him. Didn't you question his intent?"

"Uncle Russ provides me with a place to live for a very low rent. He also has power over me. He beat me when I was younger and he has connections. He could easily have me killed if he wanted that. I chose not to ask questions. If the police charge me with abetting a murder, I'll get a long prison sentence. Even abetting the possession of fentanyl can get you ten years."

"Maybe not. Aunt Kay is a criminal lawyer and she's allowed to practice in Arizona. Don't know if she could represent you but maybe she could point you in the right direction. A lawyer could work out a deal for you. You provide the information that the police need, and the police agree not to prosecute you."

"Can I think about it?"

"Of course."

"Deb, since I'm seeing you now, I assume we don't need to meet up tomorrow? But, if you're up to it, we could walk over to the diner now. I'll buy supper. And if you think I should talk to your aunt about representing me, I could drive us to the hospital after."

"Okay, that sounds good. I need to call Aunt Kay before we go and get myself together. Would you mind waiting for me in the lobby. I'll be down shortly."

As soon as he was out the door, she clicked off the recorder. Then she called Joey.

-19-

JOEY ARRIVES

"Hi, Debra," he answered. "Are you okay? Where are you?"

"I'm in my room. Where are *you*?"

"I'm here in Cottonwood. Flew down earlier and rented a car. I sent you a text message, but you didn't respond, so after I checked in, I went to the hospital and saw Kay. She said you met with the sheriff and all was set for tomorrow. We must have just missed each other. I'm in my car and about to leave now."

Then she noticed the text she had missed. "I'm sorry. I was asleep and missed your text. I see it now. Joey what room are you in?"

"Room 208 just down and across the hall. Are we good for dinner?"

"Joey, Eddie showed up at my door while I was asleep and woke me up. We had a long conversation and I got him to confess to buying fentanyl and to implicate my mom and Russ in the murder. He may be willing to tell everything to the police if they agree to not charge him with a felony. It's all on the recorder you gave me. He's waiting for me in the lobby. He's taking me to dinner and then to the hospital to see Aunt Kay. You're okay with that aren't you? I will be at your door after I get back. I really need to be with you tonight."

"Debra, I'm concerned about your safety. I don't want you to end up hurt, or worse. Are you sure you can trust him to take you to dinner and then the hospital and not to his uncle?"

"I think so, Joey."

To Joey, she didn't sound that sure.

Joey considered tailing Debra and Eddie that evening, but decided that would be a bit overboard. Nevertheless, he was very relieved when she banged on his door after she returned just before ten.

"Debra come in. I'm so glad to see you," he said as she entered. She rushed toward him and put her left arm around his neck, but winced as she attempted to do the same with her right arm. Her forehead pressed against his nose, but the neck brace kept her from looking upward into his eyes and kissing him on the mouth. He instinctively placed his hands on her hips. She winced again and burst into tears. "Are you alright? No, you're not, are you."

"Joey I'm so glad you're here. I wanted to hug you and kiss you properly. I'm frustrated that it hurts and I can't do that. I'm sorry."

"It's okay." He relocated his arms behind her back, bent his knees and lowered his body until their lips met. Then he gave her a long gentle kiss on her mouth. "Is that better?" he said softly.

"Yes," she said with a slight giggle.

He straightened up and held her for several moments before he spoke. "The past twenty-four hours must have been a terrible experience for you. What is the latest? You told me that Eddie was taking you to dinner and then to see Kay at the hospital. Are things okay between you and Eddie? He didn't do anything to you did he?"

She chuckled. "No. Eddie was a gentleman. He didn't hurt me or take me to his uncle. But getting him to tell me all he knew and then convincing him to talk with Aunt Kay took a lot out of me. Aunt Kay recommended a local lawyer that can represent him if he turns himself in. I really hope he does that."

"Perhaps my concern was a bit over the top. I just didn't know where things stood."

"It's okay. It's why I love you. Joey, I'd like to be with you tonight. I mean, not—"

"It's okay," he smiled. "I understand."

"Look, I haven't fully unpacked yet. Perhaps it would be easiest for you if I just bring my bag and laptop over to your room."

She agreed and he followed her down and across the hall to her room.

Once in her room, she readied herself for bed, took a pain pill and got comfortable under the covers. Meanwhile, he busied himself uploading the recording of her conversation with Eddie onto his laptop. He also copied the recording onto a flash drive that she could give to the police. By the time he was ready for bed she was sound asleep. He kissed her on the forehead and then got into the other bed—the one originally intended for Aunt Kay.

-20-

VISIT WITH MOM

Debra slept until mid-morning and when she awoke, Joey was no longer there. He had left a note for her. He said that he needed to make some business calls and then he was going to the hospital to see Kay. He would give Kay a copy of the recording she made of Eddie. He said he would leave it up to Kay to talk with the detectives. He said the recorder was on the desk for her to use, and wished her a good lunch with her mom.

Debra had mixed feelings about the conversation she planned to have with her mom. Her relationship with her mom had become strained after she kicked Dad out of the house. Then after his death, she had been suspicious that her mom may have had something to do with her dad's murder. After his death, the police had interviewed her. She had told them everything she knew at the time— conversations she had overheard between her mom and Russ, information she had seen on her mom's computer, etc. But what she knew was not enough to even justify a search warrant. She hoped her mom was innocent, but if she wasn't, she needed to know.

As planned, Debra met her mom in the hotel lobby, just before noon. They greeted each other politely. Her mom asked how she was doing, how was Aunt Kay treating her, and what was new. "I'm getting along very well with Aunt Kay. I've always liked her. I passed my nursing exam and I'm now a licensed registered nurse. I plan to start a job at the Abraham East Side Clinic in Albuquerque on April the first."

"I'm very happy for you," she replied, but there was a hint of sadness in her voice.

"How are *you* doing Mom?"

"I miss having you here, and with all that has happened recently, I've been feeling depressed."

"I'm sorry Mom. I'm here now. We can talk."

Debra's finger lingered on the switch of the recorder before she pulled it. *Do I really want to betray my mom? What if Eddie was lying about what he saw? But then again, I can record now and decide later what to do with it.* She switched the recorder on while they were in the car, but her mom said little until after they arrived at the Coyote Diner. They sat in a booth for relative privacy. After they ordered, they began to talk openly about their relationship.

"Mom, you said you are depressed. Are you still seeing the therapist?"

"Yes, I am."

"How is she helping you?"

"She is helping me to understand my *feelings,*" she said with an air of indignation. We talk about my *feelings* for Dan, my *feelings* for Russ and my *feelings* for you. She even has me keeping a diary of my feelings. Every time I have strong feelings about something that happened, I'm supposed to write it down and then when I see her, we're supposed to talk about it. What's the point?"

"Mom, you had strong feelings for Dad. You hated Dad, didn't you?"

"Yes, I did."

"Mom, surely you understand that I cared about him. His death has been very upsetting to me. Do you hate *me* for that?"

"No, I don't hate you for that, but I did hate your father for what he did to us and I don't regret kicking him out."

"What did he do, Mom? I want to understand."

"What did he do? He was sexually fondling you. Isn't that enough?" she said excitedly.

Debra looked around. Fortunately, no one seemed to have overheard. She took a breath and let it out slowly. She needed to stay calm.

"It wasn't what it looked like. He was upset after finding out about your relationship with Russ, and I was also upset because I had just broken it off with Eddie. We were consoling each other."

"It wasn't the first time, was it? He had consoled you before that, hadn't he?"

"Mom, we never did anything that wasn't mutually consensual. I cared deeply for Dad. He never violated me. We hugged a lot. We expressed our feelings."

"Is that what you called it? I think he groomed you and was taking advantage of you. I couldn't let him do that to you."

Debra didn't respond to that. She realized that if she was to get any useful information from her mom, she would need to keep her own emotions in check.

"Mom, things weren't right between you and Dad before that. I want to know what happened between you and Dad."

"You're right. It happened over several years and there were multiple things. One of those things was him telling you that we weren't your biological parents. Apparently, when you were volunteering at the hospital, you talked with a patient who said he had worked with a Steve Johnston before his tragic death and wondered if you were his daughter. So, you went to Dan for an explanation. That's when Dan told you that we adopted you and that we were not your birth parents. I was furious with him for telling you that. I didn't want you to know that I wasn't your birth mother, and I didn't want you searching for her. We argued about that."

Debra recalled that long before that, there had been clues. Once a student in elementary school had asked her why her skin tone was tanner than that of her parents. On another occasion, her Aunt Kay had taken her shopping and the sales clerk had commented on what a lovely daughter she had. It didn't mean anything at the time, but after learning that she had been adopted, Debra became more curious. She tried to get her birth record from the hospital. That's when she learned that her birth record and her adoption record had been legally sealed. She decided she may need to live without knowing who her birth mother was, but one question persisted to this day.

"Mom, why . . . why didn't you want me to know who my birth mother was?"

"I was afraid that if you knew, I might lose you. We signed legal papers that prevented us from revealing it."

"Mom, it doesn't matter that you're not my birth mother. I will always consider you to be my mom. You wouldn't have lost me."

"Well, I appreciate your saying that but there's more. I always wanted to be a mother but I couldn't have kids of my own. When we adopted you, we thought that Dan was sterile, but later we found out that it was me. When I finally managed to become pregnant, I miscarried. We tried again to no avail. We couldn't afford invitro or special hormones. We finally gave up."

"I'm sorry mom. I didn't know. You had adopted *me*. Didn't you try to adopt again?"

"Yes, but the agencies turned us down. We had money issues. Your father was out of work after his bank failed. And then he tried to start a finance and loan company that went under. Your aunt stepped in to help with the expenses, but I resented that. I expected your father to man up, but he got depressed and lost interest in sex and in me. He told me we were too old to have more kids."

"But why did you get involved with Russ?"

"I needed something more in my life. I became active in your PTA, and that's when I first met Russ, and that's how you started dating Eddie. Eddie probably snitched on me about Russ and you probably told your father. It all went downhill fast after your high school graduation. Your father told me that if I was going to have sex with someone else that maybe he would also. He told me that he was disappointed that he never had the chance to father a child biologically. And he said he told you that. Then I saw him in bed with you. I had this sudden fear that he was going to father a child with you. . . It made me want to kill him."

"Yes, and you said that you wanted him out of my life and that if you ever saw him with me again, you *would* kill him. **Isn't that what you said?**" Debra caught herself getting emotional and toned it down.

"Yes," her mom responded weakly. "I was so angry."

"Mom I'm sorry, but I assume you shared all of this with Russ?"

"I did. He was so understanding and comforting. He said he would do anything for me."

"Mom, I need to tell you something. I had dinner with Eddie last night. He told me that you and Russ are not seeing each other anymore. What happened?"

"Until recently, things were going great between us. He even proposed to me." Debra's face registered surprise.

"Did you say yes?"

"No. I told him I was married. He said I should get a divorce. I told him, I was working on it, but it would be a long and drawn-out process. He asked, 'why, is there a lot of money involved?' And that's when I told him about the terms of the estate and the insurance policy that would only pay off if one of us died while we were still married. He said, 'It sounds like you might be better off if he was dead.' And I said something like, 'You're probably right about that.' Of course, I never meant that literally."

"Mom, Eddie told me that he thinks his Uncle Russ did it. He thinks Russ murdered Dad. Is that why you and Russ are no longer seeing each other?"

After Debra said this, her mom turned and looked hard at her. "I never thought he was serious, but over the holidays he seemed to change. He kept asking about the insurance payout. I told him the authorities ruled it a homicide, and the insurance company wasn't going to pay until they knew who committed the murder. He started acting like he was more interested in the money than in me. So maybe he did do it."

"How could Russ have done it?"

"Well, as the maintenance supervisor, he had a master key to all of the apartments."

"Mom, you know I discovered his body, right? It was horrible. I found Dad on the floor. His face was blue. He had attempted to reach the wall phone and had fallen. He was clutching the phone in his left hand. His head must have hit the counter as he fell. There was dried blood on his forehead. He had foam oozing from his mouth. **It made me scream and then I cried. I still have nightmares.**" She lowered her head and clasped her hands over her face.

"Debra, I'm so sorry. I wanted to protect you; I never wanted to hurt you—I mean I didn't even know that you had been seeing him." Debra considered her mom's words. *Did she just admit that she had asked Russ to murder Dad? And she must have known I was seeing him.*

Debra recalled the exchange she had with Russ the Thursday before Dad died. She had arrived at her dad's apartment in the early afternoon. Dad had given her a key so she could be there when he was at work. She found his place to be perfect for her online studies. It was quiet, and unlike her home in Cornville, his location in Cottonwood offered excellent high-speed Internet service. When she arrived, she had encountered Russ and they had talked.

"Hello Debra. Do you come here often?" he had said mockingly. "Your mom doesn't want you to be here, you know."

"I suppose you will tell her."

"No need. She already knows," he had responded.

Then she had asked him why he was in the apartment. He had made up a story about investigating a water leak— later proven false. He had no work order or other legitimate reason to be there.

As she told Eddie the day before, she had reported every detail of this encounter to the police.

After a few moments, she stopped thinking about her encounter with Russ and returned her attention to her mom.

"Mom, I didn't need you to protect me. What I needed was to feel loved. I know you told me you never wanted me to see him again, but he was my dad, and we cared deeply for each other. I often went to his place. Russ saw me there. Surely you knew."

"No, Russ never told me you were seeing him," she said, apparently lying. Debra wanted to call her out, but restrained herself.

"Mom, the police think that the Thursday before Dad died, Russ planted a poisoned capsule in his Nutri-Balance bottle. Then when Dad put capsules from the bottle into his weekly pill box, he unknowingly included the poisoned capsule."

"Sounds like a stretch. How could they ever prove that?" she asked. "When we first heard he was dead, we thought it was a heart attack or a stroke."

"Well, when I saw his body, my training as a nurse told me it was more likely poisoning than it was a heart attack. I saw his pill box. He had taken his Nutri-Balance capsule, the first thing he would do before breakfast. It was from the previous day. He had been dead for more than a day when I found him. I saw dirty dishes and unfinished coffee on the kitchen table. He had taken his capsule, finished his cereal and had gotten dressed, but his coffee was unfinished. The timing made sense. It would have taken about twenty minutes for the capsule to dissolve in his stomach. Apparently, he had tried to reach the telephone, but collapsed onto the floor before he could punch 911. I didn't think he would have died that suddenly of a heart attack. He recently had his annual physical and had shown me the results. He had no issues. I concluded that his capsule contained poison, and after I talked with the coroner, he agreed to rule the death suspicious."

"It would have been much simpler if he hadn't done that."

"What do you mean?"

"Well, now there's a murder investigation, I'm still waiting for my insurance payout, and Russ and I broke up. And to top it off, I know you think I may have been involved."

"Were you involved?"

She didn't answer but kept talking.

"How can they prove anything? They didn't find fentanyl in any of his capsules, did they?"

"No, they didn't." *Did the news media report that the poison was fentanyl? The medical examiner only reported publicly that ingested poison was the cause of death,* Debra recalled. "But Mom, if Russ did it, how would he know that Dad was taking Nutri-Balance capsules?"

"Well, unfortunately I told him. Russ said he was feeling run down, and I mentioned that Dan had been taking Nutri-Balance and it seemed to help. I suggested he might want to try it. He said he would, so I ordered a starter package and gave it to him."

"I see. But Mom, you work in a pharmacy. Explain how Russ could have put fentanyl into one of the capsules. Wouldn't it require a great deal of skill to replace the contents of the capsule with fentanyl? And how do you even get fentanyl? Eddie says that you can't get small amounts of fentanyl in powdered form. He says you would have to get tablets and crush them into powder to fit inside the capsule. And how do you pull those capsules apart anyway? Do you think Russ would know how to do all that without help?"

"Those are good questions. I don't have all the answers, but I can say that Russ is no dummy. He could have figured it out."

"Mom, why do you think Russ would do it?"

"For my money?"

"Do you think Russ did it?"

"Maybe."

Debra picked up the tab and her mom drove her back to the Inn.

"Debra, I'm glad we had this visit." her mom said. "I missed you and it was good to see you again. I'm glad we talked. The investigation hanging over me has been hard for me to handle. I need it to go away."

"Mom, however things play out, I'll always love you," Debra responded. Then they hugged each other and parted company.

Debra realized that her mom may be a murderer and that she may have helped to expose her. She wondered if she really meant it when she told her mom that she would always love her. Perhaps she only felt sorry for her. She had tears in her eyes as she watched her mom drive off.

She clicked off the recorder and returned to her room. Joey was not there. She called his room. He was not there either. She no longer felt the stress she had felt before she met with her mom. The meeting had gone as well as it could have, she surmised. She took two Tylenols, laid on the bed, and had no trouble falling asleep.

-21-

TOGETHER AGAIN

Debra awoke suddenly to the sound of voices and the door slamming closed. She sat up to find Joey and Aunt Kay standing before her. Aunt Kay had her left arm in a sling, a brace on her wrist, and visible bruising on the left side of her forehead.

"Oh my gosh, you're back!" she exclaimed. "Aunt Kay, will you be okay?" she asked as Joey helped her onto her bed.

"The doctor told me it would take a while, but I'm glad to be here rather than there. How are *you* doing?"

"I'm doing much better," Debra responded. "Aunt Kay, do we need to let Detective Logan know that tonight's meeting with Eddie is off?"

"No. He called me this morning and I told him that Eddie met with you yesterday and canceled tonight. I also told him that you and Eddie came to see me last night and that Eddie might want to talk after he gets himself a lawyer. Detective Logan says he wants to meet with us again before we leave town, so I agreed to a meeting tomorrow morning at nine-thirty." She paused. "Joey told me you recorded your conversation with Eddie. Do the police know this yet?" She sounded annoyed.

"No, they don't. Did Joey explain why this occurred?" Joey defended himself by moving his head up and down from across the room. Then Debra said, "Aunt Kay, I think the three of us should have a conversation as to what we do next. You should listen to the recording and advise us on its legality and its value, and then we can decide on how to proceed."

"Exactly what I told her," Joey declared.

"Okay, you guys, I hurt and I'm not in a good mood right now. Give me an hour to rest, and then we can do it."

"I'm going to my room," Joey said. "I can stay with you Aunt Kay."

"No, it's okay. Go be with Joey. I'll be fine."

Back in Joey's room, Debra told Joey about her meeting with her mom and that she had recorded it. Joey uploaded the recording onto his laptop and copied it onto a new memory stick.

Two hours later they went back to Aunt Kay's room and the three of them talked about the meeting they would have in the morning. Aunt Kay listened to the recordings and decided that nothing on the recordings incriminated Debra. She recommended that they give both recordings to Detective Logan. Debra and Joey agreed. Joey gave Debra a goodnight kiss and retired to this room. He understood Debra's need to be with Aunt Kay.

***

The next morning the three of them got up early, packed their bags and checked out of the Pioneer Inn. They got into Joey's rental car and he drove them to the Cottonwood police station, where they met with Detective Logan and Lieutenant Armstrong. The detectives were pleased to receive the recordings of Eddie and Debra's Mom. Joey was unhappy that the detectives wanted his recording device as well, but he gave it up without a fuss. It was close, but they made it to Flagstaff in time for their flight home.

Shortly thereafter, the three of them landed at Albuquerque's International Airport, gathered their luggage and were on their way to the parking lot. Joey pulled Aunt Kay's bag with one arm and his own bag with the other. They were back home at last. It was only 5:30 in the evening, but it had been a long day, Aunt Kay and Debra were not pain free, and they were tired. But they had accomplished their mission,

They arrived at Aunt Kay's car first. While Joey busied himself loading Debra's and Aunt Kay's luggage into the trunk, Debra asked if it was okay if Joey came to their place for dinner. She offered to cook. Joey overheard and offered to help.

"Okay we'll wait here until you have your car and you can follow us home," Aunt Kay stated.

Then as Aunt Kay proceeded to open the driver side door, Debra shouted, "**Whoa, Aunt Kay. You are not driving! I will drive us.**" Joey, smiled as he walked toward his own car. Kay had determination. Debra had initiative. He found both equally impressive.

Debra pulled Aunt Kay's car up the short driveway and parked alongside her own car in the carport, and Joey pulled his car up behind her. Aunt Kay's house was typical of the other houses in her development. It was a single story ranch style with three bedrooms on a quarter acre of land. Aunt Kay had kept the master bedroom for herself and used one of the smaller bedrooms as a home office. After relocating various items that she had stored there, the third bedroom became Debra's room. Aunt Kay and her husband had purchased the house about twelve years ago after she had established herself as a local attorney. The house had been well maintained; the marriage had not.

After entering the house, Aunt Kay got comfortable on her living room sofa while Joey and Debra took over the kitchen. Aunt Kay was a good cook and her kitchen was her domain, but she was too tired to protest. Debra prepared a side salad while Joey prepared a chicken and rice dish with a mushroom and green olive sauce. An hour later the three of them sat at the table to eat. Due to their respective conditions and Joey's abstinence, iced water replaced white wine. They raised their glasses and Joey proclaimed, "Mission accomplished!"

***

Aunt Kay's physical condition improved and she resumed her practice at her law firm. Debra had begun her new career as a registered nurse working for Doctor Isaac Abraham at his new East Side Clinic. She loved her job. Debra needed to focus on her own life now. She pushed all thoughts about her father's murder conspiracy to the back of her mind. Debra continued to see Joey on weekends. Usually, she would stay with Aunt Kay during the week but would come to Joey's house after she left the clinic on Fridays and stay until Sunday morning and sometimes evening.

-22-

JUSTICE SERVED

Justice moved fast over the next two months. Susan kept Debra informed and mailed her copies of the local news as the case progressed. Eddie had done the right thing. He went to the police. He had information about the Dan Johnston murder that he had not shared with them earlier. He hoped they would not charge him with a crime, for withholding information, for abetting a murder, or for helping to purchase a drug used in a crime. If they did charge him, he hoped to trade the information he had about the guilt of Uncle Russ for a lesser charge. The charge of abetting a murder was a class one felony and could result in the same penalty as first-degree murder. Eddie wanted to avoid that. The police had the recording that Debra made, but they did not reveal that to Eddie and his lawyer. The prosecution wanted more than a recording made by a third party. If Eddie testified to everything that was on the recording, and if Debra also testified, it would be powerful. So, they reached an agreement with Eddie's lawyer.

Eddie agreed to testify in court to everything he knew about Russ's and Debra's mom's involvement in the murder. However, on advice of his lawyer, Eddie did not reveal his role in the purchase of the fentanyl. The only evidence of that was on the recording, and the police didn't think it was enough to charge him. The police considered charging him with obstruction, but technically they couldn't prove that either. In his prior interview with the police Eddie had not lied, but simply claimed the right not to self-incriminate. Unless Eddie died or reneged on his promise to testify, the police had no need to reveal they had a recording.

Debra's recording of Eddie implied that he helped Russ. However, the police found no evidence that Eddie had used Russ's computer to place the order. And they found no evidence that Eddie handled the package when it arrived in the mail. They did not file charges against him. He had spent six hours at the police station. Although they did not arrest him, his interview did draw attention—a couple paragraphs on a back page of the Verde Valley Independent. The article suggested that Eddie was under investigation for the Johnston murder. In a small town word spreads fast. Eddie did not return to Russ's house after he left the police station. He took a week-long vacation from his job and left town. When he returned, he moved in with Susan.

Susan kept Debra informed of the latest events. She told Debra that Eddie had confided in her that he did not use the drug and did not knowingly participate in the murder of Dan Johnston. She told Debra that while Eddie sometimes made poor decisions, she thought he was basically a good person. Debra agreed with that assessment. Susan said Eddie had temporarily moved into her place. Susan said she loved him and would support him.

Debra had wondered if Eddie would be safe. She remembered that he had expressed fear of his Uncle Russ, and now she wondered if Susan would be safe. However, her fears subsided when she learned from Susan that the County Sheriff's Department had served search warrants and removed evidence from Russ's house. The news made the front page of the local newspaper and was also on the local TV news. But the news also appeared in the Prescott's Daily Courier and Flagstaff's Arizona Daily Sun. According to the news articles, the County Sheriff's Department took Russ's cell phone and his desktop computer as well as multiple documents. They also obtained call records from the phone company and search history records from the Internet service provider. The evidence showed that someone used Russ's computer to order Fentanyl and that he paid for it through a third-party bill processer, like Pay Pal. Russ's name was on the order, the credit card, and the shipment address. This evidence, combined with Eddie's and Debra's testimony, was more than enough. Sheriff deputies arrested Russ Gotti in early April and charged him with the first-degree murder of Dan Johnston. Due to the seriousness of the charge and the fact that others may have been involved in the crime, the court denied bail.

While the prosecution had a strong case against Russ, they would only have a circumstantial case against Debra's mom. However, they thought they had enough evidence against Russ to get him to plea bargain in exchange for what he would say against Debra's mom.

Debra wondered if the police would arrest her mom next. She called her mom to get the latest information. Her mom told her the police had already called her in for another interview.

"Mom, do you think they will charge you with something?"

"Apparently Russ has been telling them that I planned your father's murder, and they want me to confess, but I'm not going to do that. Russ misunderstood what I said to him and acted on his own. I didn't do anything wrong!"

Debra knew it was only a matter of time before they charged her. It upset her to know that her mom could be that manipulative and have no remorse about the consequence. She told Aunt Kay about the phone call and how she felt.

"Your mom could be manipulative," Aunt Kay told her.

"What do you mean?"

"I'm sorry. I shouldn't be critical of your mom."

"My mom probably killed your brother. It's okay if you want to be critical. How was she manipulative?"

"Well . . . you remember when I graduated from law school? You were seven years old at the time. I had invited the three of you to my graduation ceremony. It was a big deal for me. Your father called me the morning they were to leave home and told me they couldn't come. He said your mom had become ill and was vomiting and she needed him to stay with her. And of course, he obliged. I was very disappointed."

"I remember that. I was disappointed also."

"Well later, your father told me that she had taken Ipecac and made herself vomit. He said she kept a bottle of it in the medicine cabinet in case you had an issue when you were younger, but they never needed it. After my graduation he found that the bottle was only half full."

"My mother really didn't like you, did she?"

"No, she didn't."

"Why? What happened between the two of you?"

"Someday I'll explain, but not today."

Aunt Kay seemed to get teary eyed. "Aunt Kay?"

"You know I love you, Debra."

She couldn't remember her mom ever telling her that.

"I love you too Aunt Kay."

The two of them hugged.

-23-

AN INVITATION

Toward the end of April, Debra received a letter in the mail from Susan. It was an invitation to a wedding. Susan and Eddie were getting married. Susan wanted Debra to be the Maid of Honor, and allowed her to bring one guest. The wedding was to be on the first Saturday in June. Not much time ahead she thought. She would need to check her schedule and she had so many questions. She called Susan on the telephone and they talked for probably an hour.

"When exactly?"

"The ceremony will be on Saturday afternoon at five-thirty, and dinner and dancing will follow. However, I would like you and Maria to be with me from around noon, so that we can get ourselves ready."

"Maria?"

"Maria is my other bridesmaid. She's someone I work with. Don't think you ever met her."

"How big a wedding will it be?"

"Maybe fifty people."

"What do I wear?"

"Give me your dress size and your shoe size and I'll have your dress and shoes ready for you the day before the wedding."

"Where will it be?"

"The wedding will be at The Ranch on the outskirts of town. And the rehearsal and dinner will be the night before at a restaurant in town hosted by Eddie's Uncle Jim. He's not sure which one yet."

After many other questions and answers, Debra asked the big one.

"Why so soon? I mean it's only five weeks away."

"Because I'm three months pregnant," she said matter of factually. "Will you be bringing Joey. I'd like to meet him. You told me he's quite a dancer. Tell him there will be dancing at the wedding reception. I think he will enjoy it."

After she hung up the phone. Debra began to think about her history with Susan. Susan had been her best friend, certainly the one she had known the longest. The Smythe family had moved to Cottonwood when she and Susan were in the third grade. Her parents, Dan and Kate Johnston had become friends with Susan's parents, John and Mary Smythe, through work. The families often got together socially. She and Susan had attended the same middle school and high school in Cottonwood. After the school day she had often gone home with Susan where they either played or studied together. Her father, Dan, worked in Cottonwood and after work he would pick her up at Susan's house and drive home to Cornville. In high school she and Susan were on the softball team together and they were both good players. While Susan was in the drama club and was the homecoming queen senior year, Debra was class President and an honor student. Eddie was Debra's boyfriend in high school and he had taken her to the Senior Prom. But later when her interests turned to college and preparing to become a nurse, Eddie became involved with Susan. She remembered how upset she had been when she found out. But eventually, she agreed that Eddie was more suited to Susan than to her. She forgave them and the three of them remained friends. Susan and Eddie did not go on to college, but both had good jobs in the Cottonwood area. Now, Susan Smythe would marry Eddie Gotti and she would be Susan's Maid of Honor. She couldn't wait to tell Joey. She called him.

"Joey, there's something I need to tell you. Susan told me she's getting married to Eddie. They set the date for the first weekend in June. She asked if I could be there, so I called her and requested more details. I asked why so soon—only five weeks away. She said she's pregnant but still wants a proper wedding, which her parents will provide. She asked if I could be her Maid of Honor. I told her I would let her know."

"You probably should do it. The two of you are long term friends, right?"

"Right. And she said that I could bring a guest. Would you want to come with me?"

"Of course."

"I'm also remembering that I have belongings at the house in Cornville which I'd like to retrieve. Do you think we could do that as well?"

"If we take an extra day and drive there, we could go to your mom's house before the wedding. I'm assuming I have enough room in my Lexus for whatever you intend to bring back."

"Yea, I'm not talking furniture, just books and clothes."

"I'll look forward to it then."

***

A week before the wedding, Debra received another communication from Susan. The news was not good. Debra's mom had been arrested. She was being held in the county detention center without bail, pending trial. Susan provided a link to the news article. They charged her with first-degree murder, conspiracy to commit murder, and a few lesser charges. Debra reported this to Aunt Kay, and later that evening she talked with Joey.

"What exactly is happening," he wanted to know.

"Mom was arrested," she said. "I just found out from Susan today. As you know, Russ has been in jail. They probably gave him the option to plead guilty to a lesser charge and testify against Mom, and they may need that. Three days ago, I received a letter from Mom. She said the Sheriff's Department raided her house and she expected them to arrest her. Yet, she still thinks a jury will find her innocent. She repeated what she had already told me. She claims that Russ misunderstood what she said to him and that he took it upon himself to kill Dad. The trial date is not yet set but will probably be in the late Fall. They might both be better off if they plead guilty to a lesser charge. If they are guilty of first-degree murder, they will face the death penalty, or at least life without parole. And, if it goes to trial, I will probably have to testify. I don't look forward to that but nothing I can do about it. Even if Mom pleads guilty, I may still need to go to the sentencing."

"I'm sorry Debra. You've been through too much. I will support you anyway I can. Perhaps we can visit her when we go there for the wedding. I'm willing to go with you for support if nothing else."

"I appreciate that."

"Not a problem."

-24-

HOUSE IN CORNVILLE

Joey picked up Debra at Aunt Kay's house at eight in the morning on Thursday. They drove the 400 miles to Cottonwood, Arizona and checked into the Pioneer Inn.

Debra and Joey were up early Friday morning. There would be a rehearsal dinner that evening, and Debra would meet with Susan and the wedding party prior to that. But that left the morning and early afternoon open. They used the opportunity to drive to the house in Cornville and retrieve the rest of Debra's belongings. Now that Debra's mom was in prison, the house was under the supervision of the Sheriff's Department. Kay had arranged with them to allow Debra to legally remove her personal belongings as listed. That included clothing, books, memorabilia, trophies, diplomas, and oh yes, a pool cue stick given to her by her dad. Joey and Debra drove the ten miles from the Pioneer Inn to the other side of the mountain and pulled into the driveway of the house in Cornville that Debra had grown up in. A sheriff's deputy greeted them, list in hand.

The house was a large twentieth century ranch style house, typical for that region of the country. A living room, a large kitchen with pantry, a dining room, a small office, and one bath were at the entry end of the house. Down a long corridor toward the other end of the house were four bedrooms, another bath, and at the very end, a room that had become Dan's recreation room. The recreation room included a full-sized pool table. Debra commented that originally the Johnston family managed a cattle ranch and a subsistence farm with 50 acres of land. But by the time Debra lived there, only ten acres remained and the only outbuilding still standing was a large shed. The shed served as a garage, equipment storage area, and a workshop that Dan had created for himself. After Dan's death, Debra's mom auctioned off all those tools and equipment, as she had no use for them.

After the deputy let them enter the house, Debra led them to what had been her room only seven months prior. The room was large. A double size bed extended from the back wall along the wall to the left. A clothes closet was on the back wall to the right of the bed. A student desk was on the front wall immediately to the right of the door. A bookcase and a dresser were along the wall on the right. Strategically placed scatter rugs topped the wide old-style floor boards. The room looked comfortable. Joey unfolded two storage boxes and set them by the door, while Debra removed an old suitcase from the closet and heaved it on top of the bed. Debra loaded clothes from her closet and dresser and Joey began to load books from the bookcase. The sheriff's deputy stood uncomfortably idle in the hallway.

Satisfied that everything was under control, the deputy announced that he was going to step outside for a few minutes to have a smoke. "Call me if you need anything," he said as he left. Debra took advantage of the opportunity. She went into her mom's bedroom and returned carrying a couple of books with a large thick book on top.

"Add this to your box Joey."

She set what she had on top of the books already in the box. Unfortunately, the deputy had returned just in time to see her exit her mom's bedroom.

"What did you take from the other bedroom?" he demanded to know and walked toward the box of books.

Before he could get there, Debra reclaimed the large book, turned and walked toward him, blocking his view of the box of books.

"My mom borrowed one of my books," she answered.

"Let me see it."

"Okay," she said as she placed a book titled DRUG ALMANAC in front of his face.

"How do I know it's yours?"

"It's one the books I had for school. I recently graduated with a BS in nursing and I'm now a registered nurse. Look, I put my name on the inside. See."

Meanwhile, while Debra distracted the deputy, Joey noticed that she had also removed a notebook from her mom's room and it was now on top of the stack inside the box. He quickly placed himself between Debra and the box, and buried the notebook underneath the stack and out of sight.

"Well okay, I'm just doing my job. You're allowed to take anything that's yours. Sorry."

"Not a problem," she responded.

On the way back to the Inn, Joey asked her what was in the notebook she found in her mom's bedroom.

"We can take it inside and look at it. It's a journal that Mom was keeping. When I saw her in March, and this should be on the recording we made, she said her therapist had asked her to keep a journal of her feelings each day. Then when she met with the therapist they would talk about those feelings. I quickly scanned through it at the house. It may contain incriminating evidence regarding my dad's murder."

"Wow!" was all he could say.

Back in the privacy of their hotel room, they sat on the edge of the bed and began to read the entries in the journal. Debra read several entries out loud:

August . . . 2014

I caught Dan in Bed with Debra. I told him to leave. It was bad enough that we were having marital problems but now he is taking advantage of Debra. I am angry. I won't let him do that to Debra. I told him to leave.

. . .

December . . . 2014

Dan and I agree that we want a divorce. But he says he owns the house and he wants me out. How can he say that? Where would I go. I won't grant him a divorce if he wants to take my life away.

. . .

July . . . 2015

I learn that Debra has been going to Dan's apartment. I feel hurt. Am I losing her?

. . .

August . . . 2015

Russ and I discuss the problems I have with Dan. He is sympathetic and I feel good that he will help me. We agree on a plan. After Dan is gone, Russ and I will share the money and the house. I look forward to being happy again.

. . .

September 30, 2015

Russ says the fentanyl is ready. I go to his house with capsules and tools. We spend hours in his den. Then I go to his room for the night. He says he will handle the rest. Russ makes me feel secure. I am excited about the good things to come.

. . .

October 6, 2015

A deputy sheriff comes to the house and tells me that Dan has died of an apparent heart attack. I feel a sense of accomplishment, but I must hide that feeling from the deputy. I'm glad Dan's dead, but I also feel terrible that Debra was the one that discovered his body. It wasn't supposed to be that way. Russ and I thought that someone from his work would look in on him, or even a welfare checker.

. . .

October 8, 2015

The local newspaper says he died of an apparent heart attack. That night Russ and I celebrate. We make love. I feel good.

. . .

October 13, 2015

Dan's murder is starting to trouble me. Did we do the right thing? The coroner has now ruled the death suspicious and the manner of death will require further investigation. I am worried that it might come back to me. I talked with Russ. He says that if I tell my therapist that we murdered someone, she can't testify against me or tell the police. I hope he's right. Because I need to talk about it.

. . .

October 22, 2015

Why couldn't Debra just leave it alone. Apparently, she had convinced the authorities and the insurance company that the death is suspicious. The sheriff's department will delay the funeral until they complete an autopsy and a toxicology exam. The insurance company won't pay until this is settled. Russ says we should have made it look like Debra killed him. I had told him I wouldn't have done that and I disliked him for saying it.

. . .

November 14, 2015

The coroner and medical examiner released Dan's body. The toxicology report has not yet come back, but they have all the samples from his body they need. They have not yet ruled on the manner of death.

. . .

November 21, 2015

We inter Dan in his family plot in Cornville. People express their sympathy. I put on my best front. I have mixed emotions.

. . .

December 4, 2015

The coroner rules the death a homicide due to lethal poisoning. The newspaper says that Debra is cleared, but that Russ and I are possible suspects. I'm glad for Debra, but now I'm nervous they will prove we did it. Russ says to keep my mouth shut and ask for a lawyer if the police call me in.

. . .

January 2, 2016

Debra leaves to live with her Aunt Kay. I feel like she's turned against me. I feel lonely.

. . .

January 3, 2016

I call Russ for support. Russ and I got into an argument on the phone. He accused me of misleading him into thinking it would look like a heart attack. I blamed him for screwing up the drug purchase and causing a police investigation. I wanted his support, but now all he cares about is protecting himself, and the money he won't get. We broke up. I'm pissed.

. . .

March 08, 2016

My daughter came to see me today. She took me to lunch. She says she loves me, but I also think she knows what I did.

. . .

April 8, 2016

I'm brought in for questioning. They want information they can use against Russ. I don't think they have a good case against me. I feel relieved when they let me go without arresting me.

. . .

April 15, 2016
   Russ is arrested and held without bail. I hope he doesn't talk.
      . . .
May 05, 2016
   Two sheriff's deputies come and search my home. They take my computer and phones. They also interrogate me. But they don't arrest me. I don't think they have a case against me, but I am worried. Don't know what they would find on my laptop. I thought I deleted everything.
      . . .
May 12, 2016
   I am losing all my friends. They treat me like a leper.
      . . .
May 20, 2016
   I saw my therapist tonight. I told her how depressed and anxious I feel. We talked about my options: turn myself in and confess; end my life; flee; or wait to be arrested. I chose the latter, at least for now.

"That last entry was only three days before they arrested her. Joey, this does not look good for Mom. **She's guilty as hell! I hate her!**" Debra looked down and put her hands aside of her head as the reality of the situation hit her.

"You alright?" Joey asked and put his arm over her shoulder.

"It's what I expected and yet I was hoping it wouldn't be true. But it is. They could execute her over this . . . unless—"

"Unless you destroy the diary? They may have enough evidence without it. That's why they arrested her. It's your choice, but destroying evidence is a crime."

"Yeah, you're right. And she deserves what she gets. Let me call the deputy and see if we can drop it off at the police station."

"A wise choice."

-25-

PRISON

Aunt Kay had arranged for Debra to visit her mom in jail at 1:00 p.m. The Yavapai County Detention Center was only twenty minutes away in Camp Verde. As required, they arrived fifteen minutes beforehand. After they signed in, an escort led them to a visitation room where they would have a video visit.

"Why a video visit?" Debra asked the escort. This was not what she had expected and not what she had seen in the movies or on TV shows. She had expected to see her mom in the flesh.

"It's something new and it's for security reasons. No need to transfer prisoners between buildings," the escort replied. "If you have any problems with the equipment, raise your hand and I will come help."

Joey and Debra took seats in front of a large screen monitor. Partitions on either side gave privacy from other visitors in the room. Joey observed more than a dozen other video stations in the room. Using the touchscreen, Debra entered the appropriate information into the computer. A few moments later, Debra's mom, Kate Johnston, appeared sitting at a small table from somewhere inside the jail.

"Mom, how are you?"

"I'm fine. Who is this?" she asked as she saw Joey for the first time.

"This is my boyfriend, Joey."

"Boyfriend? He looks like he's as old as I am. You can't replace your father you know."

"Mom, that was mean."

"Sorry. Just so the two of you are happy together. That's what's important."

"Mom, you look gaunt. Are you eating and sleeping?"

"I'm doing my best. The food is terrible and it's not easy to sleep. This place does things to your mind. Can't wait to get out of here."

"Did they deny you bail?"

"May as well have. It's set at two million dollars."

"Have you considered pleading to a lesser charge and maybe get immunity if you testified against Russ."

"I don't think I'm guilty. Russ misunderstood my feelings and he did this. If it goes to trial, I'll get off. I told my lawyer I don't want to plead guilty."

"Did your lawyer tell you that Russ might take a plea and get immunity in exchange for testifying against *you*?"

"They don't have a case against me."

"Mom, if Russ testifies, I think they have a strong case. If you're found guilty in a trial, you could get the death penalty. You need to listen to your lawyer." Debra considered telling her that the police had her journal, but thought better of it. Perhaps her mom's hope of an acquittal would keep her spirits up.

"If I take a plea, I still might get twenty years. The death penalty might be better than living in a prison like this for twenty years."

"Don't talk like that. Stay positive. Mom, before I left home you were seeing a therapist. Do you still see her?"

"I was until they arrested me. Why?"

"I was wondering if seeing her might help you adjust to prison life and stay positive."

"She called me and plans to talk to me again on Tuesday— Have you been to the house yet to get your stuff?"

"Yes, we have. The sheriff's deputy let us in. The house is fine."

"You didn't come all this way just to see me or get your stuff at the house. What else is going on?"

"Susan is marrying Eddie tomorrow. I'm the Maid of Honor. The rehearsal is later today."

"Is Eddie staying off drugs?"

"I think so Mom."

"Before they locked me up, I heard Susan was pregnant. Good thing you broke it off with Eddie. Could have been you, you know. Too bad Russ won't be there. Serves him right."

They talked for a few more minutes before their time was up.

"Mom, our time is up and we need to be going, but I need you to take care of yourself, and listen to your lawyer and your therapist."

"Thanks for coming. Tell Susan I wish her the best. I always liked her."

Debra started sobbing before they even got back to the car. She was clearly upset. Joey held her tightly.

"Talk to me."

"Seeing my mom like this is very upsetting. On the one hand I hate her but on the other hand I feel sorry for her. She's not in her right mind. She thinks she will get off. She refuses to admit what she did, and plead to a lesser charge. She's going to get the death penalty. And she seems depressed. I don't think she will last in prison. I'm scared for her welfare."

"Debra, you've done everything you can. You're no longer responsible. You must leave it in God's hands."

"Joey, didn't you tell me that you no longer believed in God?" she asked, raising her voice.

"No, I told you I no longer go to church. I still believe in God. Debra, your mom's therapist should be able to assess the situation and do something about it. Okay?"

"Yeah, she should. Sorry I yelled," she said as she regained her composure.

"Debra, I need you to keep it together. Think about Susan's wedding and share in her joy."

They hugged, got into the car, and headed back to Cottonwood.

-26-

REHEARSAL

Susan and Eddie had scheduled the wedding rehearsal for later that afternoon. A rehearsal dinner would follow. Susan, Debra, and Susan's other girlfriend Maria planned to meet prior to the rehearsal. According to Debra, the ladies would have last minute preparations and details to talk about. Joey would not be part of this, so he agreed to drop Debra off at Susan's apartment and see her later at the dinner. He didn't mind. It was Friday so after he dropped her off, he used the opportunity to make some business calls back home.

Meanwhile, prior to the rehearsal, Susan and Debra had time to talk privately. They talked about their current activities and about their plans.

"Susan, last time we talked, you mentioned that you were changing jobs. What is it that you do now?"

"Three weeks ago, I began working for Century Real Estate in Cottonwood. I just got my real estate license."

"Congratulations. I hope you do well at that."

"Although I haven't made a sale yet, things are looking good so far. I enjoy the work and the hours are flexible. That flexibility will be more and more appreciated as this develops," she said as she patted her tummy. She paused. "Debra, could I ask you something?"

"Sure."

"Do you think I'm doing the right thing by marrying Eddie?"

"Susan, are you having doubts? It's not like you. Why?"

"That's just it. I've always made quick decisions. I don't always think things through like you do. If I did, I wouldn't be pregnant."

"Well, if I were you, I would marry him. Even if you weren't pregnant, it's normal to have last minute doubts before you get married. At least that's what I'm told."

Susan paused as if unsure she should ask,

"Debra, you told me that before you broke it off with him, he got rough with you. Do you think he could hurt me?"

"Well, he did get rough with me, but he didn't hurt me. After I told him I didn't want to be intimate with him, he got very frustrated. He threw me onto the bed and tried to force me into having sex with him."

"What did you do?"

"I talked him out of it. I told him that he made his choice when he hooked up with you, and I was not going to be part of a threesome. But I also told him I cared about him and wanted to stay friends and that you had told me you really liked him and I thought the two of you would be good together. Did he get rough with *you*?"

"No, but he can have a temper."

"Well, you will never know everything about another person, but for what it's worth, I think you should marry him."

"Could I ask about you and Joey?"

"Sure,"

"Do you think you will marry him?"

"I don't know. We've only been together for about five months and there's a lot I still don't know about him. As you know, he's twice my age and has a lot more life experience. His wife died in a car accident almost a year ago and her death was suspicious. He also has a past, a life prior to 2005 that he won't talk about. On the other hand, he's super smart, good looking, and an excellent dancer. He's very supportive, but not controlling, and he treats me right. He's great in bed, and I think I'm in love, but until I know more, I'm just enjoying the relationship and seeing how it all plays out."

"He sounds like a great catch to me Debra!"

***

Later in the afternoon Debra and Susan joined the rest of the wedding party at the Rustic Ranch just outside of Cottonwood where tomorrow's wedding and reception would take place. A wedding coordinator stepped them through the details of the ceremony—who would sit where, who would escort who, where the minister would be, where each person would stand, what they would say, and so on.

Tonight's rehearsal dinner was at a local restaurant in town, known for hosting rehearsal dinners. Joey arrived at the restaurant in late afternoon and made his way to the doorway of the private room where the dinner would take place. Debra had told him earlier that attendees would include those who were in the wedding party plus their spouses, significant others, parents, and guardians. In addition, the minister may also attend.

Joey stood at the doorway and peered in. Only two people were in the room. Apparently, the wedding party had not yet returned from the ranch. He was early. Inside the room he saw a large middle-aged man talking with a female member of the restaurant staff. So, he walked in and asked if he was in the right place for the Gotti rehearsal dinner.

"You with the wedding party?" the man asked.

"Yes," Joey responded.

"You're in the right place. I'm Jim Gotti," the man said. "And you are?"

"Joey Ramirez. You must be related to Eddie."

"I'm Eddie's other uncle. Russ is my brother. He was Eddie's guardian. He can't be here so I'm his proxy. How about you. You have a horse in this race."

"I'm with Debra Johnston, Susan's Maid of Honor."

"Well, you can't be her father or her brother. You her bodyguard?"

Joey turned and faced him head-to-head. "Why would she need a bodyguard?"

"Cause, she might be in danger. When she was here three months ago, someone ran her off the road and tried to kill her."

"What do you know about that?"

"Only what I read in the local news. It said she was supposed to meet with someone in the Sheriff's Department the next morning. Suggested that she might be working with the police to investigate her father's murder."

How would the local news have known that, he wondered.

"Did the police try to find who it was that ran her off the road?"

"They may have tried but Debra and her lawyer couldn't give them much to work with," Gotti responded.

How would Gotti know that?

"So, you think that Debra is still in danger?"

"Saw my brother this morning. He told me that the prosecution may ask Debra to testify against him. He says her testimony could really hurt."

"Interesting. Do you think your brother would try to harm her? If he did, he would be making it clear that he was guilty. Don't know if he would want to do that, do you?"

"He would if it looked like an accident or suicide."

"It almost sounds like you're making a veiled threat."

"No threat. I'm just giving you a head's up about what I've heard. Look, if she testifies, she will be subjected to cross examination. I've heard that her father molested her, so she and her mother both had a motive. They will make it look like she and her mother did the crime.

Look at it this way. If she refuses to testify, it's a win-win. My brother gets off, Debra avoids humiliation in court, and she no longer needs you to protect her."

"Well, what I've heard is that they have an iron clad case against your brother, even without her testimony. I hear that Eddie may have to testify against him."

"No way Eddie would say anything that would hurt Russ."

Joey remembered the recording that Debra made. Apparently, Jim had no knowledge of it.

"Jim, your brother faces the death penalty. Maybe he would be better off taking a plea and agreeing to testify against Debra's mom. That way your brother would get a lighter sentence and stay alive. And, Debra wouldn't need to testify. And then there's the possibility that Debra's mom might take a plea and testify against your brother. Again, no need for Debra to testify."

"Well, if that happens, it would be best for Russ if neither of them testifies. I hear bad things can happen to people in prison. . . Just saying."

"In my opinion," Joey responded, "they are both guilty and they should both plead to a lesser charge. That would save them from the death penalty and it would also save the cost and aggravation of a trial. To me that would be a win-win for everyone."

"Don't think that will happen," Jim replied.

Just then a lady approached. Compared to Jim's large frame she looked petite. "Jim, don't mean to interrupt, but we should go talk with Eddie. She spoke in a soft voice and didn't even look at Joey."

"Okay Virginia. Tell Eddie I'll be there shortly. I need to stop in the men's room first" Then he turned to Joey. "Please excuse me, Joey. We'll talk more later."

Debra showed up less than a minute after that.

"Joey, come. I want you to meet my friends before we go to dinner."

She led him into the room where Susan and a few others had gathered.

"Susan, I'd like you to meet my boyfriend, Joey Ramirez."

"Pleased to meet you," she said. "You're even more handsome than Debra described."

"It's a pleasure to meet you, Susan. Debra tells me you guys were best friend in high school."

"And we still are," she responded.

Just then, another young lady appeared holding a drink in her hand. "Susan who is this?" she asked.

Susan put her hand on Joey's arm. "Joey, this is my other best friend from high school. Maria, this is Joey. He's Debra's boyfriend."

"Boyfriend?" She looked surprised. "I'm sorry. You look older than what I expected," she said tactlessly.

Joey laughed it off. "Yeah, I get that a lot."

"Joey, let's go meet Eddie," Debra said and led him over to a bar set up in one corner of the room.

Eddie was nursing a beer while talking with his Uncle Jim. Virginia stood by but wasn't saying anything. As they approached, Jim and Virginia left.

"Eddie, I want to introduce you to my friend Joey." She purposely avoided the term boyfriend after hearing Maria's reaction.

"Hello sir," Eddie responded and extended his hand and received a friendly shake. "My Uncle Jim is convinced that you're Debra's bodyguard."

"What?" Debra said and gave Joey a quizzical look.

"Oh, no Eddie. Your uncle misunderstood. I'm just her friend," he said realizing the sensitivity of the term boyfriend.

"It's okay Joey. I knew that. Susan had filled me in."

"Did you tell your uncle?"

Eddie chuckled. "When Uncle Jim gets something in his head, there's not much point to arguing. I let it go. Hey, can I get you a drink, Joey? They have a good IPA here."

"No. I'm good, but thanks."

"Oh guys, I think my uncle is trying to get our attention."

Once he had everyone's attention, Jim Gotti let everyone know that he was sponsoring the rehearsal dinner on behalf of the groom and his brother Russ who couldn't be there. Then he explained the procedure for dinner. There was a buffet table set up along the back wall. The caterer was bringing in the food as he spoke. "Sit wherever you wish," he said. "Help yourselves to as much food as you wish. Plenty to go around. You're welcome to sit anywhere." He also let everyone know that wine, beer, or soda was also available at no charge.

Joey noticed that the room had four tables set up with five chairs each, but there were only sixteen people at the dinner. When Joey and Debra returned from the buffet table with their meals, they took a seat at the table with Susan's parents and the minister. Joey was pleased that Jim Gotti and Eddie decided to sit at another table. John and Mary Smythe had been friends with Debra's parents, Mary and Dan. They were very cordial and Joey enjoyed the conversation. Joey and Debra told the story about how she and Joey met in a snowstorm and Mary told Joey how Susan and Debra first met in middle school. Mary asked how Debra was doing in New Mexico. Debra talked about how much she was enjoying her new job as a nurse and mentioned that she was living with her Aunt Kay who grew up in Cornville. Mary mentioned that she had met her aunt at Dan's funeral. Joey told everyone what he did for a living and John took an interest in what he said. John was a bank manager and said they might need a new security system at the bank. The two even exchanged business cards. John talked very favorably about Dan, who had also worked at the bank. John said he was upset when he heard that Dan had died, and was very disturbed when it was determined that his death was a homicide.

"Despite what your mom accused him of doing to you, he didn't deserve to die that way," John stated. His comment earned a disapproving glance from his wife.

"No, he didn't!" Debra spoke up. "And for the record, what my mom accused him of doing is not true." Joey put his hand on the back of her shoulder to calm her.

"Oh, no, of course not. I didn't mean it that way," John said apologetically. "Please forgive me. When that rumor started, I asked Dan about it. He denied it, and I believed him. Dan was a good man."

"It's okay," she said as she relaxed. "But I don't want that rumor going around." She looked at others at the table who had overheard. "It's not true."

"This whole thing must be very hard on you. I want you to know that we support you," Mary said.

The conversation then returned to more pleasant topics and John even offered to get Debra another glass of wine which she accepted. Later, when it was time for the evening to end, they hugged. John told Joey he enjoyed their conversation, and Mary gave him a hug and said she was pleased that Debra had found someone like him.

On the way out the door they thanked Jim Gotti for sponsoring the evening. "See you tomorrow," he said to Joey. "Remember what we talked about earlier. Let's hope the right people win in the future." *Another veiled threat?* Joey wondered.

On the way to their car, Debra asked, "What is it that you and Jim Gotti talked about earlier?"

"Oh, nothing important. Just politics. But I did find him rather interesting. We were talking before you guys came back from the rehearsal. We would have talked longer except that Virginia came to fetch him and tell him they needed to talk with Eddie. And right after that you came and got me. I never had a chance to ask him what he did for a living."

"He owns a car and truck repair service—just down the road on the outskirts of town. He also has his hand in a few other things, and he's a city council member."

"What about Virginia? Does she work for him?"

"His wife? Oh no. She works at the police station. I think she's a secretary."

"Do you think that Jim and his wife could have had something to do with your car accident?"

"I never considered that. Why would you think so?"

"His wife could have given him inside information about your trip to Cottonwood and your reason for coming. He had small trucks at his disposal and he had the motivation to protect his brother. In other words, he had means and motive. And the newspaper article after the accident had information about why you were in town. How did they get that? And if Eddie was privy to information that the police planned to have you wear a wire, it might even explain why Eddie decided to meet with you a day early."

"Well, given who Jim and Virginia are, it's unlikely that they will ever be investigated."

"Yeah, you're probably right about that."

Joey started the engine and they headed back to the Inn.

-27-

POMP & CIRCUMSTANCE

Like the rest of the weekend, Saturday's weather was perfect for an outdoor wedding. The day would be sunny and dry with a light breeze. Temperatures would peak below ninety degrees and the humidity was less than thirty percent. The wedding was not until late afternoon, so they had the morning to themselves. They decided to enjoy the pool. They were able to swim a few laps before it got too crowded. After Joey climbed out of the pool, he watched Debra as she continued doing breast strokes the length of the pool and back. He marveled at how perfect her strokes were and how fast she moved. He also marveled at how attractive she was in her two-piece swimsuit as she climbed out of the pool. She was aware of the attention he was giving her and she gave him a big smile.

"Where did you learn how to swim like that?" he asked when she returned to their lounge chairs.

"Thought I told you. I was on a swim team during my high school years. A couple of the trophies I took from the house were for swimming."

"They were lucky to have you," he exclaimed.

When they returned to their room, he kept thinking about how sexy she looked, and more than an hour went by before they showered, dressed, and had brunch.

The Rustic Ranch was a twenty-minute drive to the north side of town. As planned, Joey and Debra arrived three hours before the wedding. The ranch offered an ideal place to hold a wedding and a reception. Joey and Debra walked from their car to a structure called the barn. The barn was where the dinner and dancing would take place after the ceremony. It had a room where Susan, and her two maids could change and ready themselves. Susan and her mother were already there when Debra arrived. Joey said hello to them and left them to do their thing.

For the next three hours, Joey busied himself doing a crossword, checking out the grounds, taking photographs, and talking to people as they arrived. The marriage ceremony would take place outdoors in a location designated as the chapel. Joey followed a long stone-paved walkway that led from the barn to an outdoor altar. Behind the altar was a large scenic tree that provided a cooling effect on a hot day. Off in the distance he could see mountain ridges. As he neared the altar, he passed folding chairs set up on the grassy area on both sides of the walkway. For this wedding, twenty chairs on each side would be enough. Joey photographed the scene. Then Joey walked back up the walkway to the other side of the barn until he came to a fence. On the other side of the fence, he saw horses wandering in an open field. More photos. Eventually, people began to arrive, and he claimed a seat on the right side of the walkway in the second row.

It wasn't long before Eddie and the minister took their places at the altar and the sound system began to play appropriate music. Joey took pictures as Jim Gotti escorted important people to their seats. Susan's first maid Maria arrived at the altar, escorted by her male counterpart. Then Debra arrived, escorted by Eddie's best man. The maids wore pale blue sleeveless V-neck A-line gowns matching shoes, chic updo hairstyles, and makeup. Joey had never seen Debra look this gorgeous. He took at least three camera shots and Debra gave him a smile as she passed by. Then after what seemed like ages, Susan's father John escorted Susan down the walkway to the altar. He looked proud and Susan seemed happy. She had a rather simple bridal gown but it was loose fitting around her waist and gave no indication of her pregnancy. After taking as many camera shots as he could, Joey retreated to his seat and the ceremony began.

While the minister was speaking and while the bride and groom were saying their rehearsed vows, Joey's mind began to drift. He pictured standing with Brandy in a similar outdoor venue when they had married, four years earlier. Then he pictured standing at the altar with Debra.

Thoughts ran through his mind. *Should he consider marrying Debra? Would she even consider marrying him if he were to ask?* He wondered if she loved him that much or was it just infatuation? She had a long life ahead of her, he not as much. Long term, would it be in her best interest to marry him? Perhaps she could have a better life with someone else, someone her own age so that they could experience new things together. He wouldn't want to hurt Debra the way he had hurt Brandy. He had broken her heart years ago and then almost seven years later they had met by pure chance and rekindled their love, only to have it end tragically last year. He had been to therapy and knew he was not directly responsible. Yet he knew that if it had not been for him, she would still be alive. He would always feel some guilt. He didn't want to do that all over again with Debra. When he heard the words, "I now pronounce you husband and wife," he snapped out of it, and watched the two of them kiss.

After the ceremony, he made his way to the receiving line. He congratulated Susan and Eddie and wished them a fruitful marriage. When he got to Debra, he whispered in her ear that he had never seen her look so gorgeous. He told Susan's parents he thought they did a wonderful job and deserved a lot of credit. Near the end of the receiving line, he told Jim Gotti and his lady friend that they should be proud of Eddie and that he wished Eddie the best.

-28-

DINNER & DANCING

After the photographer took many pictures, everyone went into the barn for dinner and dancing. It was a large structure. Perhaps it had been a working barn at one time; perhaps not. If so, it no longer looked like one inside. The owners had removed evidence of any stalls and lofts that may have existed. At each end of the structure, they had added restrooms and rooms where wedding participants could change clothes and primp. For today's event, a buffet table was on one side of the barn and a platform for a band and a wine and beer bar on the other. Forty-five people were in attendance and eight tables with tablecloths were available near the buffet. The floor of the barn was a brown colored masonry. Not ideal for dancing but it would do.

Susan did not want the bridal party to sit at their own table isolated from everyone else. She wanted to encourage conversations between people who may not already know each other. Debra and Joey sat at a table with bridesmaid Maria and her guest, Michael, and another couple who had come in from out of town. During dinner, the six of them talked freely and got to know each other. Joey was not shy and he enjoyed talking with people he had just met—after all, he had been a salesman. He spoke with Maria who sat to his immediate right and learned that she also spoke Spanish, and this led to more conversation between them.

After the meal, the band began playing and Susan and Eddie were on the dance floor for the first dance, a waltz. They had obviously practiced and did quite well. After Susan's father had his turn, everyone joined in. Debra enjoyed waltzing with Joey. Before they came, she had never danced a waltz. She wasn't sure if she could do it, but Joey had spent time with her at home in preparation and she learned quickly. While dancing, Joey told her she did very well and he enjoyed dancing with her.

"Are you enjoying the wedding?" she asked him. "You're not bored, are you?"

"Not at all. I've enjoyed being here with you and I've enjoyed talking with your friends."

"I'm pleased that you are getting along with everyone. My friends seem to like you. I wasn't sure that would be the case when I first invited you, but you fit right in. I noticed that you struck up a conversation with Maria. I don't know her that well. Is she interesting?"

"Yes, she speaks Spanish so we have something in common."

They returned to their table and talked some more. Meanwhile the band began playing Latino music. Joey asked Debra if she wanted to try it, but she declined. This was Maria's favorite music. After Maria realized that Michael was not into it, she asked Debra if she would mind if Joey danced with her. Debra said she didn't mind and of course Joey willingly obliged.

"*Pero no quiero hacer una bachata sensual*," Joey said lightheartedly to Maria as they arose from the table.

"*Entiendo,*" Maria replied.

First, the band played a fast salsa. Maria proved to be an excellent dancer, as skilled as he was, he thought. People began watching them. Then the band followed with a slower bachata. Joey thought for moment. Maria had agreed there would be no sensuality but didn't say she wouldn't do a bachata. So, they began. In a bachata, it's the female partner that expresses most of the emotion and often sensuous feeling. The longer they danced the more feeling and emotion Maria expressed and Joey had no choice but to accommodate. Their dance was by no means indecent, but at times it was suggestive. By the time the music stopped they had an audience, and the audience applauded. When they returned to their table, Debra was not there. Before they sat back down, Michael told them that he thought that their dancing may have embarrassed Debra and that she had politely excused herself and headed for the ladies' room.

Joey asked Maria for help. "Please, Maria would you mind going into the ladies' room and talking to her."

"Okay. Joey, I'm sorry. Perhaps I got carried away out there. I'll see what I can do."

While he waited, he talked with Michael. "You didn't have an issue with my dancing with Maria, did you?"

"Oh no. I thought it was an excellent performance. You are both excellent dancers."

"Did Debra say anything to you before she left the table?"

"She asked if it bothered me to see you dancing like that with Maria. I told her no. I told Debra that Maria and I have been friends for a long time and I've watched her dance on numerous occasions. It's her thing and she's good at it."

"Thanks."

Joey made his way to the rest rooms and intercepted Debra and Maria as they exited.

"Debra, we need to talk."

"The two of you embarrassed me. I want to leave."

"Joey, I tried to apologize, but she's too upset. I need to get back to Michael," Maria said and walked off.

"Debra. I'm sorry. I had no intent of embarrassing you. I let the dance get out of hand. I should have made her stop. I'm sorry . . . but, please hear me out. I have a suggestion that will restore your dignity."

"Really?" she said doubtfully.

"I want you to walk over to the band with me and ask then to play your favorite slow dance piece. And then I want us to dance together. I want everyone to know that you are above this and that we love each other. You will come across as strong and forgiving, and you can hold your head up high. There will be nothing for you to be embarrassed about. Please, if not for me, do it for yourself."

After a pause, "Okay."

The band complied and they danced closely together, doing a slow country waltz. Others joined them on the dance floor. When the music stopped, he kissed her and they hugged. While still on the dance floor, Maria and Michael came over and Maria apologized to Debra again.

"Debra, please forgive me." She sounded sincere.

The two of them hugged. Others took notice. All was forgiven. No one thought the lesser of them as the band resumed playing.

***

On the drive back to the Inn, they barely spoke. When they were back in their room and in their night clothes, Debra went to the other bed and sat on the edge. She was obviously still upset. Joey sat beside her, put his hand on her shoulder.

"You're still upset with me, aren't you?"

Her response surprised him. "I think I'm even more upset with myself. This isn't the first time I've had this kind of a reaction. When I see you having a really good time with another woman, this feeling comes over me."

"Is it the same as when I danced with Aunt Kay at your birthday dinner?"

"Yes. And I know I shouldn't feel that way but I do."

"Can you think of other times when you have had similar feelings?"

"I had those feelings when I caught Eddie together with Susan."

"You got over that, didn't you?"

"It took a while but I did. Eddie and Susan remained my friends. Dad was especially supportive and then when Dad died, I got those feelings again. When I saw him dead, and later at his funeral, it was almost more than I could handle. But Aunt Kay helped me through it. I really needed her. Then I got those feelings yesterday after our visit with Mom and then again today at the wedding."

"Can you see a pattern here?"

"I'm not sure."

"You lost people in your life that you needed, and it traumatized you. Then when your subconscious mind fears that it could happen again, you get that feeling. For example, when I danced with Aunt Kay, you subconsciously feared losing both of us. And today, you feared losing me . . . subconsciously."

"What do you think I should do about it?"

"An important first step is recognizing it for what it is. I think you've just done that."

"I feel like I need you and I don't want to lose you."

"You're not going to lose me."

"I need you to make love to me." She pulled him down onto the bed and he obliged.

-29-

RELIGION & POLITICS

The next morning was bright and sunny. They packed up the car and got a quick breakfast at the nearby diner. Back in the car, Joey looked over at Debra with a serious look.

"Debra, today is Sunday and I know you often go to church on Sunday. If you want to do that, I'd be willing to go with you this morning before we hit the road. Cornville is on the way to the Interstate."

What he said surprised her, considering his words the day before.

"I thought you gave up on church?"

"I did for myself, but if it's something you need, I want to support you."

"No, I appreciate your sentiment but it's not necessary. Dad, Mom and I often went to a protestant church in Cornville, but to be honest, I haven't been there since Mom kicked Dad out of the house."

"But you have been going to church with Aunt Kay."

"Yes, but primarily to please her. You know, I don't think you and I are that far apart as far as church is concerned. And besides, I wouldn't want to subject us to the inquisitions that would occur after the service. It would take a lot of extra time as well. No, Joey, it's okay. I think we should head home."

"Okay. Home it is."

Debra set her half-finished coffee in the holder between the seats, flicked on some soft music and settled back in her seat.

They were about halfway home when the skies darkened and it began to rain. Debra removed her sunglasses and looked for a place to put them. Empty coffee cups filled the center console and there were papers and who knows what in the center shelf below the dash. Then she opened the glove box in front of her thinking she would set them in there. This got Joey's attention.

"Debra, what you doing?"

"Looking for a place to temporarily store my sunglasses."

"Ahh—" He started to reply but he was too late. She had already reached into the glove box with her eyeglass case in hand. As she attempted to insert the eyeglass case into the glove box, she realized that it would not fit. That prompted her to peer inside to see if she could make room. What she saw was unexpected.

"Joey, you have a gun?"

"I do. Please don't mess with it."

"I wouldn't think of messing with it. I hate guns. Why do you have one?"

"It's fully licensed and legal—"

"I'm sure it is, but you didn't answer my question."

"I have it for sport and for protection. It sounds like you don't approve."

"Sport? You mean you hunt and kill innocent animals?"

"No, I don't hunt, and for what it's worth I've never killed an innocent animal."

"So, what do you kill? People?"

"Debra, stop. Shooting is a sport like bowling, golf, or archery. I go to the shooting range once per month and shoot at targets. They rate me based on how well I do."

"And you said you use it for protection. Protection from what?"

"Well, it could be that someone might try to hold me hostage in exchange for the schematics or the security codes of a system that I've installed. Or if someone tries to mug me or hijack my car with me in it, I might use it to dissuade them. I also have a second gun at home. I have two because Brandy owned one. If someone were to invade my house and threaten me with physical harm, I might use it then."

"I don't think I'm comfortable with what I'm hearing."

"Well, for what it's worth, I've never had to shoot anyone."

"That's good."

"Debra, I don't understand something. Your dad grew up on the farm in Cornville. Didn't he own a gun?"

"The Johnstons kept a twenty-gauge shotgun on the wall by the rear door. It had been there for generations. Dad never used it. He told me he hated guns. When Mom kicked him out of the house, she said she would use it to blow his head off if he didn't leave by morning."

"Now I understand the nightmare you had that first night in Flagstaff."

"Guns scare me."

"Well, they *should* scare you. And you shouldn't handle one unless you've been properly trained. Both Brandy and I were NRA certified instructors. We took turns teaching an eight-hour course, Gun Handling and Safety. When you complete the course, you get an NRA certificate. I highly recommend it even if you never own a gun. However, these courses are going online now, so I may not teach this course again."

"Doesn't the NRA think everyone should have a gun?"

"No, they don't, and neither do I. But I do think that everyone who is a *law-abiding citizen* who is *not mentally ill* has the *right* to own a gun. I also believe they should complete background checks *before* one takes possession. And I think you would be surprised that many people you know might own a gun."

"Like who?"

"Well, two years ago, I saw your aunt at the firing range. She had lost interest in me when she learned that I was married, so we didn't speak, but she was there."

There was a long pause. "Perhaps I'm overreacting. I'm sorry."

"Don't be. It's okay if we have different viewpoints, so long as we can discuss them."

"I think I'm still trying to figure out what my viewpoints are . . . and I'm still trying to figure you out as well."

"I think you know by now that I'm less than perfect. But let me ask you this: if I *were* perfect, would you still love me?"

She chuckled. "Probably not."

-30-

MOM'S DECISION

Debra had a busy week after returning from Cottonwood, including a full shift the following Saturday to make up for lost time. She spent Sunday with Aunt Kay. They went to church and then went to a church picnic. Joey understood her schedule and she would plan to see Joey again the following weekend. When Debra came home from work on Monday, Aunt Kay said she had an important phone message. She should call Detective Logan with the Yavapai County Sheriff's Department. It would be after hours for him, but it was important, so she went into the other room and called right away, only to get his voice mail. She left a message and Logan returned the call only minutes later. He informed her that a guard found her mother dead in her jail cell that morning. The death appeared to be suicide. The news was stunning. Debra recalled her visit and that her mom seemed depressed, but never thought she would do this to herself. Detective Logan was very professional and apologized for needing to do this by phone. He also asked if she was okay and if anyone was there that she could talk to. She told him yes. Then Logan told her that her mom had left a note. In the note, her mom said she was sorry for the hurt she caused and could only hope for Debra's forgiveness. Logan said he would mail her a copy.

After Debra hung up, she noticed Aunt Kay standing nearby.

"Debra, what's wrong? Are you okay?"

"Mom is dead. She killed herself."

"Oh, Debra I'm so sorry," Aunt Kay said as she embraced her.

"Do they have any idea how she was able to do that?"

"They said it looks like strangulation, but that's all they would tell me."

"Debra, are you going to be okay?"

She told Aunt Kay she would be okay and could handle it. It was one more downer in her life. Debra had mixed feelings. On the one hand, she had loved her dad, and her mom had killed him, so good riddance to her. On the other hand, Mom was remorseful for the hurt she caused, and she had been a decent mother for most of Debra's life. Debra said she would come to terms with it and put it behind her. Aunt Kay gave her a hug.

"Debra, I'm here for you."

"Thank you, Aunt Kay. I love you." She called Joey and told him the news.

"Mom killed herself," she said. He could hear the sadness in her voice.

For a moment Joey recalled what Russ's brother, Jim Gotti, had said to him before the rehearsal dinner. *Could she have been murdered?* But he kept the thought to himself. His speculation ended when Debra said her mom had left a note, the coroner had ruled suicide, and Detective Logan had agreed.

"Debra, I'm so sorry," he said. "Please let me know if I can help, or if you just want to talk."

"I'll be okay Joey. I hope to see you on Friday and we can talk more."

Then she called the family lawyer and talked about the will and handling the bills. Her mom had been true to her word—Debra would inherit everything. That included the ten-acre farm and the house and outbuildings. Debra arranged for a cremation of the remains, but she could not decide what to do with the ashes. Her Mom had never discussed that with her. She could decide that later, but one thing was for sure, Mom and Dad would not be near each other.

Later in the week, Debra received a call from Susan. "I'm very sorry for your loss," she said. "I know you had mixed feelings about your mom, but still, I hope you're doing okay. Her death was on the local news and in the paper. I'll send you a copy."

And then she asked about the house in Cornville. "I understand you will inherit the Johnston farm. Are you thinking of selling it? If you decide to sell, I will be pleased to be the sales agent. No rush. Just let me know."

"I've already decided. I will sell, and yes you can be the agent. Send me whatever papers I will need to sign. However, I don't have ownership yet. Our family lawyer will need to handle the title transfer to me. You're welcome to contact him and work with him. I'll send you his name, address, and phone number in an E-mail."

After work on Friday, Debra went directly to Joey's house. It had been a very busy week and she needed the weekend with Joey. She hadn't seen him in almost two weeks and she was eager to be with him. He surprised her by having dinner ready shortly after she arrived. How many men did the cooking she wondered? Her mom had always done that growing up. Debra told him how lucky she was to have him cook for her and asked where he learned.

"Well, like I told you once before, I don't think I'm that good at it, but my stepmom was a good cook and then later I lived alone and learned to cook out of necessity," he said.

"I think you cook as well as my mom did. My father never cooked. Mom did it all," Debra said, "but I was never that interested. We never really connected. And now she's gone, and I'm not sure how I should feel."

"Tell me how you *are* feeling?"

"Kind of like, what a waste. How did you feel when your mom died?"

"Well, when my birth-mother died, I probably felt like you are feeling. She drank herself to death. That's like a slow suicide."

"Joey, why do people kill themselves?"

"Good question, Debra. I wonder why myself, especially if they have options. To me, suicide is not a logical thing to do. Your mom had options. There was always some chance that the court would find her not guilty, and there was always a chance to have a prison sentence rather than death. Apparently, your mom's feeling of guilt and the thought of prison life was too much of a burden."

"I received a copy of her suicide note. She pretty much confirmed what you just said."

Joey thought about his own life. He had been in more than one bad place in his life. His birth mother was an alcoholic and his father and stepmother died in a suspicious car accident. His Catholic upbringing told him that suicide was wrong. Rather than make him suicidal, his parents deaths motivated him and gave him a reason to live. He would give up alcohol and follow in his father's footsteps. He would seek social justice, and clean up government corruption.

Unfortunately, this led to his being involved with dangerous people and breaking the heart of the woman he loved. He felt guilty. Some people in his past thought he was a traitor and a killer. Many people at his church had turned on him, some of whom were corrupt government officials. He lost many of his friends and his business. If anything would have driven him to commit suicide this would have been it. But he didn't lose himself. He had gotten help from his one and only remaining friend, Ed. Then eleven years ago, he relocated to Albuquerque and restarted his life. So far, he had avoided revealing the details of his past to Debra. He wanted badly to be able to do that. But there were risks involved and he needed to be sure about how she would react before doing so. Meanwhile, Debra needed his support.

"Do you have to go back to Cottonwood to settle your mom's estate?" he asked.

"Don't think so. I've been in touch with the family lawyer. He handled Dad's death and he's trustworthy. Mom gave him an advance. He's been paying the bills and he'll take care of everything, at least for now. The lawyer says I will inherit the estate. I don't want it though, and Susan has agreed to sell it for me. The lawyer says it could be worth a million dollars."

"What about her remains. You going to bury her in the family plot?"

"No way. As soon as the coroner verifies that her death was suicide and not homicide, she'll be cremated. I still need to decide what to do with her ashes though."

"You seem to be handling this quite well," he said but secretly wondered if she was burying some of her true feelings. "But if I can help you in any way, let me know. I'm here for you."

"Joey, I feel very fortunate that I have you and Aunt Kay in my life right now. Do you have anything planned for tomorrow? You asked me to bring my swim suit."

"Well, you know, I belong to a country club. While there, I'd like to introduce you to some of my colleagues and friends. The country club also has a nice restaurant and a very large pool. I know you like to swim, so I thought you might be interested in going there tomorrow for the day. You can probably use the break."

"Sure. Sounds good. I'm in."

-31-

COUNTRY CLUB DATE

Joey had been seeing Debra for more than six months now, and it had been almost a year since Brandy had died. Debra's and Joey's weekends had been active and fun, including tennis, pool, riding on the bike, hiking, eating out, and cooking meals at Joey's house. And of course, during those weekends they shared a bed. It was all very enjoyable, but to Joey, something was missing. While Joey had his friends, and Debra was making new friends at work, most of their activity as a couple involved only the two of them. He had met many of her friends in Cottonwood, Arizona, and except for the embarrassment while dancing with her girlfriend, he thought it went well. But she had not met any of his friends from Albuquerque. Joey was concerned that as a couple, they were not socializing with other people in the Albuquerque area. Joey wanted their relationship to continue and develop. He knew that if their relationship was to develop, they would need to be more open about it with others—not just her friends, but his friends as well.

Eventually people in their lives would find out about their relationship anyway, and Joey wondered how they would react. He thought about their age difference. He already had hints at Susan's wedding that their age difference might be an issue. He wondered if his friends would think it appropriate for him to have a love affair with a young woman half his age less than a year after his wife had died. He also wondered what they would think of Debra. Would they think she was a "gold digger?' How would that affect her? He expected to see many people he knew at the country club and he would introduce Debra to them. He was pleased that Debra had agreed to spend a day there with him.

Joey also knew that if their relationship was going to be long-term, there were things he would need to tell her about himself. But he didn't feel he could do that yet. First, he needed to be sure about her commitment to him and his friends, and then he needed to judge how she would react to what he had to tell her.

***

Joey was up early that morning and was already downstairs in the kitchen when the phone rang. It was 8 a.m. and he hoped the ringing of the upstairs extension would not disturb Debra. He picked it up on the first ring, Cody was someone he was always eager to hear from. They began talking.

About five minutes later, Debra came down the stairs and walked toward the kitchen She could hear Joey talking on the kitchen wall-phone.

"Do you think the CIA will find him and get him to talk?" she heard Joey say.

As Joey listened to the answer to his question, he looked up to see Debra enter the room.

"Cody, I need to hang up now. My house guest just came downstairs."

Joey listened to Cody's response. And then, "Talk to you later," Joey said and hung up the phone.

"House guest? I'm a house guest now?" she said lightheartedly.

"Sorry about that. It was a business call."

What she had just overheard disturbed her. *A business call? The Central Intelligence Agency? What business would require the CIA to get someone to talk? Who had she become involved with?* But she said nothing. *Just one more thing he would eventually talk about,* she hoped.

"I made coffee. Help yourself. I suggest we just have cereal this morning. I'd like us to get to the pool, before it gets too hot."

***

Joey and Debra arrived at the main entrance where they signed in. As required, Joey filled out the guest information. The woman at the registration desk politely asked Debra to always display her guest pass. Joey recognized the woman who couldn't help but comment.

"Good to see you Mr. Ramirez. I see you have brought your lovely daughter with you. You have a family membership, don't you?"

"Well, Debra here is my friend. Put it on my account," Joey directed.

"Yes sir," the woman said and gave him a more than pleasant smile.

"Before we go down to the pool area," Joey said, "let me show you around."

Debra followed him down a long corridor as he pointed out the various rooms, a restaurant, a library, a lounge, meeting rooms, and finally a large event room.

"Now, they can use this room for lectures, banquets, entertainment and indoor weddings. But on a day like today when the weather is nice, the wedding would be outside." She followed him out the sliding glass doors onto a large patio. "In fact, today I think they will have two weddings out here." Beyond the patio on a well-manicured lawn, they could see a temporary altar. Two employees were in the process of setting up chairs.

"Is this where you and Brandy were married?"

"No, that was at the Sandia resort, to the north of here, but one of my friends from work got married here."

"Do you come here a lot?"

"Maybe once a week on average. Last Saturday while you were working. I came here and played a round of golf with my boss, Frank, and one of our prospective clients. Frank and his wife Ann are also members. And speaking of them, Frank and Ann have invited us to have dinner with them next Friday evening after work. You okay with that?"

"Yes. . . I hope I'll live up to their expectations."

"Don't think you need to worry."

"Where's the golf course?"

"The golf course is on the other side of the property, a short drive from here."

"Is there a fitness center?"

"Yup. Down at the other end of the building on the lower level there's the pool, a snack and drink bar, the locker rooms and the fitness center. So, what do you think?"

"Impressive. Does it cost a lot to belong?"

"Well, it's all relative. Brandy and I had a family membership, but now it's just me. I justify it because I not only use it for recreation but I also use it for business. I can meet new clients and entertain existing clients here. My company installed security systems here, and I can demonstrate some of it to prospective clients. I also volunteer my time as part of the country club's advisory committee."

She gave him a smile of approval. "Ready for a swim?"

"Let's go."

***

The two of them proceeded to the pool area—an Olympic-sized pool surrounded by an expansive patio.

"I'll meet you on the patio," he said as they went to separate locker rooms to change. Joey was first to emerge and walked toward the patio. Along the way, he passed a few familiar faces and made a point of saying hello before settling under a large umbrella with two lounge chairs and a small table on the far side of the pool. It was a sunny day but not too warm, at least not in the morning. He looked around. A fair number of people were poolside. There were two ladies he had said hello to earlier. Two guys, in their early twenties perhaps, had a table near the locker room. A middle-aged couple that lived two blocks away in his neighborhood was on one side of the pool, and a woman named Greta, who was a friend of Brandy, sat alone on the other side of the pool. He also recognized a family of four. He worked with the husband. They had two young kids with them—teenagers. He planned to say hello and introduce Debra to all of them.

He noticed Debra as she emerged from the locker room. She had a small bag in her right hand and a beach towel in her left. As she walked toward him, he couldn't help but focus on her shapely body proudly displayed by her two-piece swim suit. And he wasn't the only one who noticed. The two young guys not only noticed but also made a point of obstructing her progress so they could initiate a conversation. The conversation was short and she continued walking as the two guys continued to stare at her.

"Were they hassling you?" Joey asked when she arrived at their table. She looked at him and gave him a kiss.

"Joey, this happens to me from time to time. Trust me, I can handle it. Please don't overreact."

"I do trust you, but I'm also here for you when you need me."

"Let's go swimming," she said. Then she took his hand and led him to the deep end of the pool. They jumped in. They both did a lap from one end of the pool to the other and back, revealing their common skill to anyone who cared to watch. They were both excellent swimmers, and continued their laps for several minutes.

As they returned to their lounge chairs, they passed the middle-aged couple that lived in Joey's neighborhood.

Joey made a point of saying hello. "Jim and Linda. How are you?"

"Fine, Joey. Haven't seen you since the funeral," Jim answered. "You doing okay?"

"I'm making the best of it."

"I see that. Who is your lovely young friend?"

"I'm Debra Johnston," she quickly responded and held out her hand.

"Johnston . . . Is your mother Kathy Johnston, the criminal lawyer?"

"She's my aunt."

"Johnston has an excellent reputation," Jim interjected. "She helped my brother-in-law beat a drug charge." Linda gave him a look of disapproval for mentioning it.

"We were pleased to read that the police cleared Joey of all charges," Linda said to Debra.

Debra contained her surprise at hearing this. *Charges?*

"Joey, the paper had said her death was suspicious. Did they ever determine the cause of death?" Jim asked.

"No," Joey replied. "No one was charged. They looked for a person of interest but never found him, and they never arrested anyone. It's possible they'll rule her death an accident, but right now it's still an open case."

"Well, we all miss Brandy, but it's good to know that you're moving on with your life. Look, Jim and I are planning our annual fourth of July barbecue in our yard. I know it may be difficult for you. We will miss Brandy, but we would really like you to come. You, Debra, and Kathy are all welcomed. No need to RSVP, just come over."

"Thank you. We just may do that," Joey replied. "But let me know if we can bring something."

Joey and Debra returned to their lounge chairs and talked.

"Debra, are you okay with going to their barbecue?"

"I'm not sure. I assume there will be other neighbors and people that you and Brandy knew?"

"Yes, of course. Are you okay with that? I want to be sure that you feel comfortable if I introduce you to people who were friends with Brandy."

"What about you, Joey? Will you feel comfortable?"

"If you feel comfortable, I'll feel comfortable."

"Okay then, let's go for it. But right now, I need to go to the ladies' room. Would you like me to bring us something from the canteen on my way back—a cola, a coffee, a snack?"

"Yeah, sure. Colas would be good. Thanks."

No sooner had Debra left than Juan Cortez appeared before him. Juan was the husband who had come with his wife and two teenage kids. Juan worked for one of his clients, but they had spent time together while implementing the client's security system. Joey stood up and the two of them shook hands.

"Good to see you again Joey. And it's good to see you moving on with your life. That young lady is quite attractive . . . and young. She doesn't look much older than my daughter. Is she . . .?"

"Yes. She's my girlfriend. I've known her for six months and yes, she is young, but very mature."

"How did you meet?"

"We met in Flagstaff during a snow storm. We shared a meal and started talking. We both lost a loved one, and I know her aunt, so we had some things in common. Things just went from there."

"Well, I hope it works out for you. I need to run. The wife is expecting me to bring back some chow from the canteen."

Joey remembered the cola that Debra had promised. He looked over at the canteen. She was still at the counter and chatting with one of the young studs that had hassled her earlier. Joey watched him put a hand on her shoulder, and he watched Debra pull away. He was hassling her so Joey decided to intervene. Joey walked briskly toward the canteen on the pretense of offering to help her carry the food. Fortunately, the young stud saw him approaching and walked away before he arrived.

"Are you okay? I noticed that you had another encounter with Stud Boy."

"Ha-ha. Stud Boy? He wanted to buy me a beer. I think he already had a few. I told him no thank you, but he persisted, so I told him I was with you. Then he said you were too old for me and wanted to know if you were my sugar daddy. I told him you were my bodyguard and he didn't want to tangle with you."

"Did you really?"

"I did, and he bought it."

"I watched it all go down, and I was ready to intervene, but apparently you handled it."

"I did, but it's nice to know that you were there if I couldn't."

They talked as they walked back to their table. "Debra, he's not the first person to comment on our age difference today. You don't think it's an issue, do you?"

"Only if we let it be."

She handed a regular cola to Joey and kept the diet cola for herself.

"Let's enjoy our cola," she said and sucked up a mouthful of diet cola.

Later, they went for another swim, dried off in the sun and then decided to return to street clothes. Joey was first out of the locker rooms. While waiting, Brandy's friend Greta passed by heading toward the locker rooms.

"Hi Greta," Joey called out. "Nice day, isn't it?"

She stopped. After a moment of apparent indecision, she walked over to Joey.

"I probably shouldn't say this but I feel very strongly and I have to get it out."

"What's wrong?"

"Joey, you know I was a good friend of your wife. Brandy always told me how she adored you and trusted you. It bothers me to see you acting friendly with a sexy looking floozie half your age. There, I said it. I hope the two of you are having a nice day; I'm not."

Greta turned to continue toward the locker rooms, only to encounter Debra blocking her path. Greta gave her a nasty look and almost knocked her over as she went by.

Debra turned her head and watched Greta walk quickly away in a huff.

Then she looked at Joey with a concerned look on her face. "What happened? You look upset."

"I'll be okay. Tell you what. Let's go to lunch. We'll talk." He needed time to consider what he might say to her, not just about Greta, but about how people might react to his relationship with her. He wanted his friends to accept her, and he didn't want her to feel as if she were a problem.

***

They seated themselves in the dining room and ordered lunch. To Joey's surprise, it was Debra that initiated the discussion. "Jim and Linda seemed nice and I'm looking forward to the Fourth of July barbeque. I think it's good that we're making our relationship public. Hopefully your other friends will like me more than that woman at the pool did. When I approached, she seemed to be chewing you out, and then as she went by me, she gave me a nasty look and said, 'you can have him.' Were the two of you dating?"

"No. Her name is Greta. She was a good friend of Brandy's. They both worked at Sandia and sometimes rode together. She was unhappy that I was with you. She made some derogatory statements about you and that's what upset me." Debra looked puzzled.

"She doesn't even know me. Is there something more?"

"Well, looking back on it, I think she had a crush on me. Brandy may have confronted her on that. I'm also aware that Greta was passed over for a promotion at work and Brandy may have had something to do with that. She and Brandy may have had a falling out."

"Do you think she may have had something to do with Brandy's accident?"

"It's possible, but the police did interview her and didn't find enough evidence against her."

"So, what does she have against *you*?"

"Well, after the funeral, Greta made advances toward me under the guise of friendship. I had lunch with her once before Christmas and she told me how much she liked me. I think she was lonely. Her husband had divorced her, and she needed someone for emotional support. She continued making overtures toward me. Then, in February, I told her I wasn't interested and that if I spent time with her, I would only be thinking about Brandy—which was true by the way—because of their association with each other. I told her we could still be friends, but I wasn't interested in the type of relationship she was looking for. Her text messages to me seemed to indicate that she understood and that there were no hard feelings. But then it started up again. I told her I was seeing someone else and I didn't hear from her again, until today."

"If you were having an affair with her, you wouldn't lie to me about it would you?"

"Debra, are you having that *feeling* again?"

"Maybe."

"Look, I never cheated on Brandy and I would never cheat on you. And I've never lied to you either," he replied sternly and looked her straight in the eye.

"No, but you don't always tell me everything, do you?" she said and looked right back at him.

"Okay, where's this coming from?" he asked as he maintained his stare.

"Joey, you never told me the police charged you with killing your wife," she said in an accusatory tone while maintaining her gaze.

"I didn't, and the State Police didn't charge me! But they did investigate. Same as after the death of your dad. The coroner ruled it suspicious because he didn't think the accident injuries would have been life threatening. So, they did a complete autopsy, but didn't find anything definitive. Meanwhile, when they investigated the damage to the car, they thought a broken tie rod could have caused the accident. But they also thought that someone may have tampered with the car. So, the death was suspicious. A witness saw a man remove Brandy from the car because it was on fire, but did not know if she was conscious before he removed her. That man left the scene before the EMT's arrived and became a person of interest. They never found him. The news said he may have been an illegal immigrant who feared the police."

Everything Joey told her was true. What he didn't tell her was that the Feds knew the identity of that person of interest, but didn't want it made known to the public for reasons of national security.

"I'm sorry. I shouldn't have talked to you that way," she said and lowered her gaze.

He reached for her hand and leaned toward her. "Debra, I love you. If something is bothering you, we can talk about it."

"Okay Joey, I love you too, but I overheard the tail end of your phone call this morning. You mentioned the CIA. The Central Intelligence Agency making someone talk does not seem like a normal business call to me."

"You're right. It wasn't. The call was from someone updating me on the progress of the investigation into Brandy's death."

"And?"

"Debra, I can't say any more than I already have. For both our sakes please keep anything you overheard to yourself."

"Joey, I want our relationship to succeed, but there is so much more I need to know about you."

"I know. I'm just not ready yet. Please trust me on this."

"I'm trying Joey. I'm trying to be patient, but I'm finding it difficult. Please don't wait too long."

He got the message.

Just then, the waitress came with their meals.

-32-

INDEPENDENCE

Today was Sunday, July 3. Joey had not seen Debra since they had dinner with Frank and Ann Wilson on Friday more than a week earlier. Debra had to work the next two Saturdays to make up for her trip to Arizona. On the way home after the dinner with the Wilsons, they had talked about the evening and they both agreed it went well. Ann was Frank's second wife, and she was much younger than him. She worked as a physical therapist, so she and Debra had some common ground. They seemed to hit it off. The next day while Debra was at work, he and Frank went to the gun range. Frank wanted to know if he and Debra were having a serious relationship. Joey confessed they were, but also said he wasn't yet sure if they were ready for marriage. He explained that he wanted to be sure that she would connect with his friends.

"Well, she connects with us," Frank told him. "Ann said she really enjoyed talking with her."

"That's good to know Frank. Debra said she really liked you guys as well."

Joey looked forward to today's neighborhood barbecue. He hoped that his neighbors would also be supportive of his relationship with Debra, and he hoped that Debra would also feel comfortable with them.

Although the Fourth of July holiday was tomorrow, on Monday, Jim and Linda had scheduled the barbecue for today. Debra came over to Joey's place late in the morning. The day was warm but dry. She wore navy-colored shorts, a white tee top, a white baseball style cap, and dark shades. Her outfit complemented her tan skin. Meanwhile, Joey wore light weight pale blue slacks and a tee top with a picture of exploding fireworks on the front.

Debra let Joey know that meeting his neighbors for the first time made her a bit nervous. The neighbors had known Brandy and some knew her well. "What will they think of her replacement?" she asked.

"Not to worry," Joey had assured her. "Just be yourself. They'll love you."

Joey and Debra walked the two blocks to Jim and Linda's house and entered a side gate into the back yard. When they arrived, about two dozen people including kids were already there. Jim had set up a large canopy in the center of the yard—a wise choice for those who needed to take refuge from the bright sun. There were tables and chairs for those who needed them. Three elderly people were there talking. Straight ahead from the gate toward the rear was a four-foot deep above the ground pool. Several kids were in the pool making loud nonsensical sounds. Cornhole tossing was at the far corner of the rear. Two couples were already playing. To one side of the canopy, Jim had set up a grilling station. A thin plume of smoke rose above the canopy.

Joey led Debra to the grilling station where they announced their presence to Jim. "Linda is inside preparing potato salad, but she'll be out shortly," he said. "Drinks are over there in the cooler. A few kids and their parents are back by the pool." As more people arrived they began to mingle and Joey introduced Debra to everyone he knew. After saying things like good to meet you we're so and so, the neighbors would ask all the expected questions:

> *"How did the two of you meet?"*
> *"Where are you from?"*
> *"Where do you work?"*
> *"How long have you known each other?"*
> and so on.

Debra felt quite comfortable talking about herself and asking Joey's neighbors appropriate questions in return. But every now and then, Debra would catch a glimpse of two or three people talking, looking over her way, and then talking again. Debra found this very interesting. Obviously, they had known Brandy and were wondering about Joey's new friend. She wondered if she would pass the test. Joey had told her to just be herself, so that is what she would do.

After meeting many of the neighbors, Joey and Debra went to the grill to get some food. In between bites of brats, Joey and Jim began to talk. Another male guest joined in. Meanwhile Linda had just brought out some tacos and salsa, and had engaged in conversation with a couple of female guests.

"I'm going to say hello to Linda," Debra said.

"Okay. I'm going to talk with some of the guys. See you in a bit," Joey responded.

The guys used the opportunity to subject Joey to friendly jabs to which he would respond like:

> *"She's attractive. You are one lucky fellow."*
> *"She looks very young. Is she legal?"*
> *"Listen guys. I'm serious about her. Don't poke fun. She's a lot more mature than she looks."*
> *"Sorry man. No offense."*

Meanwhile, the female guests showed an interest in Debra, but may have been looking for gossip to spread. They asked her questions like:

"How long have you known each other? Are you in a serious relationship?"

"Will you be moving into his house?"

"Did Joey ever tell you what he and Brandy did before they came here?"

"It was never clear what caused her death. You don't think Joey could have done it, do you?"

Debra answered the best she could. "We've known each other for six months. I have no plans to move in with him. Joey did work for the government before they came here, and Brandy worked for Sandia Labs after she came here. I'm sure that much of their work was classified. But as far as Brandy's death is concerned, there is absolutely no way Joey killed her. He had an alibi, and besides, didn't they rule it an accident?"

"No. It's still an open case," one of the ladies answered. "I happen to know that before Brandy came here, she had worked for the National Security Agency. The rumor is that she and Joey were intelligence agents and that a foreign agent eliminated her. The government could be covering it up."

"You read too many spy novels," another woman told her.

Joey had told Debra that eventually he would tell her everything about his background. Perhaps it was best that he hadn't. She had no desire to contribute to the rumor mill. So, she politely excused herself in search of Joey. She found him under the canopy talking with a couple he knew.

"Debra, meet Bob and Diane. They want to know if we would like to play a game of cornhole."

"Absolutely. Let's do it."

They were halfway through the first round of cornhole when they heard hysterical shrieking coming from the nearby pool.

They looked up to see a young boy coming out of the pool.

"**Something's wrong with Tommy. We need help!**" he yelled.

Joey and Debra took off running toward the pool. Joey looked over the side of the pool and saw Tommy face down in the water with blood coming from his head. Joey immediately climbed into the pool, lifted him out and laid him on the ground. Tommy's complexion was slightly blue. Joey checked his pulse. "No pulse," he said. "Call 911," he yelled to whoever could hear. Then Joey began chest compressions and Debra began mouth-to-mouth. After what seemed like ages, Tommy's pulse returned and water and vomit oozed from his mouth. He coughed but still was having trouble breathing. Just then, Debra felt a forceful tug on her shoulders pulling her backwards.

"Get off him. I'm his mother. He has asthma and needs his inhaler."

Debra and Joey both turned and looked up. It was Greta!

"Greta, Debra is a nurse. She knows what she's doing. Please give her the inhaler." As he said this, he reached up and took the inhaler from her and handed it to Debra who placed it over Tommy's mouth and nose.

Tommy was still semi-conscious and was still having trouble breathing. He had a serious gash and swelling on his forehead. His breathing stopped again and Debra resumed mouth to mouth. She blew in and Joey gently pushed it back out with one hand on his chest. They continued this until the paramedics arrived. Then they stood up and got out of the way while the paramedics applied a legitimate respirator and transported Tommy by stretcher to the ambulance. Greta joined them and they went to the nearest hospital.

Debra and Joey looked at each other and then tightly embraced.

"He'll be alright, won't he?" he asked.

"I think so."

"You saved his life Debra!"

"We both did Joey!"

Jim came and said he was going to the hospital and asked if they wanted to ride with him. They did.

Several other guests also followed the ambulance to the hospital. Everyone waited anxiously for the news.

After what seemed like ages, a doctor came out to the waiting room and spoke to Greta. Everyone held their breath until Greta called out, **"He's going to be okay!"**

People applauded.

Then a woman with a special badge walked up to Debra and Joey.

"Hi. Are you Debra? I'm Jen Ortez, a reporter with KRQ News. I understand that you saved his life. I would like to interview you. This is Charlie, he's going to video record our interview. Can you tell me what happened?"

"Well Joey and I both saved his life . . ."

Debra told Jen everything she remembered and made sure to credit Joey for the role he played.

-33-

THE REAL WORLD

Although a holiday, Debra had to work the next morning so she went back to Aunt Kay's house for the night. That evening they shared Debra's debut on TV. The news piece totally focused on her and that she was a registered nurse at the Abraham East Side Clinic.

"That's not fair," she exclaimed. "They didn't give Joey the credit he deserved and they almost turned it into an advertisement for the clinic. "Aunt Kay, he deserves as much credit as I do. I need to call him."

She immediately called Joey. "Did you see the newscast?"

"Yes. Why?"

"They hardly gave you any credit."

"It's okay. I don't need it. This was good for you."

"And what does the clinic have to do with it? I felt like it was an advertisement for the clinic."

"Yes, but you probably didn't know that Jen Ortez is your boss's sister, and her husband has a financial interest in the clinic."

"It's not right."

"Welcome to the real world, Debra," he responded. "I agree it's certainly biased, but it's not illegal. Look on the bright side. Tomorrow when you show up at work, they will consider you a hero. Your boss increases the business at his clinic—maybe you get a raise. And everyone you met at the barbecue accepts you with open arms—a win-win!"

"I'm upset. I don't want to talk to you anymore. I'm clicking off," she said and powered off her phone, clearly annoyed.

Aunt Kay couldn't help but overhear. "Debra are you okay?"

"I'm fine. I'm just very tired. I'm going to bed. If Joey calls back, please tell him I still love him and I'll call him tomorrow night."

Two minutes later the landline rang. Aunt Kay gave Joey the message.

***

Debra laid in bed but couldn't sleep. "Welcome to the real world" is what Joey had said that rankled her. It was hard to be angry with him. He probably didn't realize what he said would annoy her. The real world? The news report was an example of how a crisis could benefit someone who had nothing to do with it. Joey was the first responder. He pulled him out of the water and restored his pulse. She just did what she was trained to do, nothing more. Joey was the real hero. He deserved to benefit, not her, and not her boss, Doctor Abraham. Did Doctor Abraham know what the news cast would say ahead of time? She hoped he was not taking advantage of her. She would talk to him tomorrow at work.

As she thought about it, she realized why Joey's statement rankled her so much. It went well beyond today's event. She had been living in the real world for some time now and in her mind, it did not always treat people fairly. She thought about how too much duplicity and too many secrets had affected her life. Yes, the real world indeed!

First there was her mom. She had a secret romance with Russ, kept her in the dark about who her birth parents were, and then secretly conspired to murder her father. Learning the truth about her mom really hurt.

And then there was Joey. He even admitted that he has a secret past. Will he ever reveal it to her? Too many questions. What did he do before he was with Brandy? Was he an intelligence agent? Was he involved in Brandy's death? What does Greta know?

And then there was Aunt Kay—was she really her aunt? There had been several clues that maybe she was her birth mother; like the maternal way she acted towards her; like their common skin coloring and their similar temperaments; like Aunt Kay's emotional display at Steven Johnstons grave; or like after the car accident when the nurse thought Aunt Kay asked if her *daughter* was okay. And what about the patient in the hospital years ago who thought Steven Johnston could be her father? There were so many unanswered questions. Why were the hospital records sealed? What happened to the husband Aunt Kay had here in Albuquerque? Why didn't they have kids?

She needed to know more about the people that were closest to her. How could she have a future with them without knowing more about them?

***

The next morning at work Debra asked Dr. Abraham about the news article. He said that his sister called to verify that Debra worked there and her position, but that he had no idea what she was going to present or write in her news piece.

"You don't have a problem with the news piece, do you?" he asked.

"I do. I think they should have given more credit to Joey. He was the real hero, not me. I only did what I was trained to do, nothing more. And I see the clinic benefiting from it, simply because I happen to work here."

"It doesn't seem fair, does it?" He sounded sympathetic. "Joey's not upset by this, is he? Look, my sister is who she is, but I swear to you, I had no knowledge that she would use the situation to promote the clinic. Wouldn't it be best if we just let it ride at this point?"

"Yes. I agree," she replied. She didn't think it was worth battling her boss over it, so she dropped it. Dr. Abraham could see that Debra was upset. He also appreciated what she had done the day before, so he gave her the afternoon off.

***

Early that afternoon, Debra called Joey and squared things with him.

"Joey, when you said 'welcome to the real world,' those words really rankled me. That's why I hung up on you. I've already been living in the real world and recently it hasn't treated me that well. My mom deceived me for more than twenty years and probably murdered my father. Then she killed herself. That's my real world."

"Debra, I'm sorry. It was just an expression."

"I know Joey, I'm not upset with you for saying it. I'm upset with the duplicity of other people and with myself for allowing it to hurt me. I had trouble falling asleep last night and decided that there were things that I could do to help myself cope. I talked with Doctor Abraham this morning. I told him I didn't think it fair that he and I benefited from the event while you got very little mention. He agreed that it wasn't fair but said he had no idea ahead of time what his sister was going to present on the news. I took him at his word and we didn't discuss it further, but I felt better after talking with him, and he gave me the afternoon off."

"That's good. Debra. Today is supposed to be a holiday. We both have the afternoon off. Do you want to come over?"

"Absolutely, but Aunt Kay has asked if she could join us in the evening. She also had to work today. Apparently, she's working on a case and needs to have it ready for court. Anyway, she suggested that she could meet up with us in the late afternoon and that the three of us could have a picnic and enjoy the entertainment and fireworks at Fiesta Park."

"Yeah. Sounds good."
"Love you, Joey. I'll be there shortly."

-34-

MOTHER

Debra drove to Joey's house and they spent the rest of the day together. They got on his bike and went to Joey's country club, where they exercised in the fitness center and went swimming.

Back at Joey's house before meeting up with Aunt Kay, Debra initiated a conversation.

"I'd like to talk with you about something that's been bothering me lately."

"Okay let's sit over here on the sofa. What's on your mind?"

"Before I fell asleep last night, I started thinking about my mom. I never understood why my mom didn't want me to know about my past and the circumstances of my adoption. In retrospect, I wish I had known, and I wish I had tried harder to find out. Anyway, I've decided that I need to know who my birth mother is and I'm not going to give up until I find out."

"Are you sure you want to know?"

"Yes. I think the more I know, the better equipped I will be to handle unexpected events."

"Sounds reasonable. But understand that knowing can be a double-edged sword emotionally. While growing up I always wanted to know about *my* birth mother. My father didn't want me to know. But after I left home, I found her. It was bittersweet because she was a drug addict and an alcoholic. I promised I would never become like her."

"So that's why you don't drink?"

"That's why. But, like I said, it can go both ways. Brandy also had a strong desire to know about her birth father while growing up. Her mother wouldn't tell her but left a letter for her postmortem. Brandy took a chance and contacted him. Turns out he didn't know about her either. Well, the two of them became the best of friends, and when she married me four years later, her birth father, Peter Troutman, walked her down the aisle. So, it can work out and I hope it does for you." He paused for a moment and he asked, "Do you have any idea who your birth mother is?"

"I think she may be my Aunt Kay."

"Hmm . . . please be careful how you handle this."

"I've been giving that some thought. I already tried to see my original birth certificate at the hospital, but was unsuccessful. I considered collecting Aunt Kay's DNA and having a lab do a DNA match, but to do that legally would require my aunt's permission. I considered snooping through her belongings while she was at work in the hope of finding some old memorabilia. But no, that wouldn't be right, and she'd probably find out. So, I'm thinking that my best option is to come right out and ask her."

"Well, you may want to consider the timing and the situation when you ask her. Maybe invite her to a dinner or someplace quiet where just the two of you can talk in private. Let me know how it works out."

That evening after the fireworks, Debra told Aunt Kay that she wanted to spend more time with her and talk about things.

"Is it about your relationship with Joey?" she asked.

"No, it's about us."

"About us? Do we have a problem?"

"No. There's no problem. I want us to know each other better. I was wondering if we could meet after work on Friday. Kind of like a girls' night out. We could have drinks and then dinner. I'll buy."

"What about Joey? Weren't you planning to go to his place Friday night?"

"It's no problem with Joey. He'll understand."

"Well, on Fridays after work, I've been going to Gabi's with people I work with, but I'd be happy to go somewhere with you instead. Did you have a place in mind?"

"Well, a steakhouse that also offers fish—I know you prefer fish on Fridays. Ruth Chris, Black Angus, Longhorn? I'll make a reservation. Seven o'clock, okay? We can meet there after work. Are you in?"

"I'm in."

***

The steakhouse was conveniently located near the Abraham East Side Clinic where Debra worked and on Aunt Kay's way home from the Johnston law office. Debra had made a reservation for 7:00 p.m. The two of them separately arrived at about the same time. They greeted each other and took a booth in a less busy section of the restaurant. After they each ordered a glass of wine, Debra started a conversation.

"Aunt Kay, we've been living together for more than six months now, and we get along quite well, wouldn't you say?"

"I would."

"I feel an unexplained affinity for you that I never felt for my mom. And going back in time, I always looked up to you, and I always felt good when I talked with you and when we were together."

"Okay."

"And recently, when we were in Cottonwood, we almost lost each other and that got me thinking about how much we cared about each other. Meanwhile I talked with Mom and realized how little I really meant to her. And now I know that she manipulated Russ to murder my father. And I have many questions like why did she do that? And I wonder why she didn't want me to know I was adopted or who my birth mother was. And why did she dislike *you* so much?"

"And you want answers?"

"Yes, and I hope you don't get upset with me for my next question."

Aunt Kay cocked her head slightly as she anticipated what was coming.

"Are you my birth mother? And why haven't you told me?" Debra's tone was not threatening or accusatory and that put Aunt Kay at ease.

Aunt Kay paused for a moment before she answered. "Yes, Debra, I am your birth mother. Until now I didn't know that you needed to know, and I was afraid of how you might react if I told you. But there was also a legal reason why I never told you." She leaned forward and reached for Debra's hand. "Debra, I hope you aren't angry with me."

"Aunt Kay, I'm not angry with you, but I want to know more about you. Aren't you really Dad's sister?"

"No. I'm not your dad's blood sister, but I was his foster sister. My birth name was Kathy Yago. My Latino parents died when I was eleven and I became a foster child. The Johnston's took me in when I was twelve and we lived at the house in Cornville where you grew up."

"So, I guess in a sense you are my aunt. Then how did you become my mother?"

"Your dad's father, Dan Senior died when I was fifteen. Your dad's brother, Steven who was only two years older than me struggled with Dan Senior's death. We had already become close and I felt sorry for him. We had sex. It was a mistake but I was very naive. I got pregnant."

"How did you handle it? Did you have to drop out of school?"

"I started my junior year at Cottonwood High School, but had to drop out after Christmas to give birth to you."

"Did you have to take care of me all by yourself?"

"No. Steven did the right thing. Steven had already graduated and had a good job in construction. He married me before you were born.

He provided financial support and his mother—my foster mother—provided maternal support for me and you, and we continued to live in the Cornville house. I thought everything would be fine until Steven died in a construction accident three months later and my foster mother got sick."

"So, what happened?"

"Dan and his wife Kate saved me. They were older and already had college degrees. They moved back into the Cornville house and took care of us. I finished my junior year in the summer and with the help of Dan and Kate I graduated from high school with the rest of my class."

"So, I don't understand. How did I end up with Dan and Kate? Did you just give me away to them?"

"No, of course not. It wasn't like that. Despite my screwed-up family life, I always did well in school. I was an honor student. The teachers and guidance counselor urged me to continue my education. They told me I had nothing to lose by applying for college admission, so I did. When I heard back that Arizona State University accepted me with a full scholarship, I was torn. It was too far to commute every day. How could I go away to college and not see you every day? Dan had become my confidant—my big brother. I trusted him. I discussed the possibilities with him. I wasn't sure what to do."

"What did he say?"

"He proposed that he and Kate should become your legal guardians. He argued that you were quite happy with them. Although I had spent *some time* with you every day, he argued that Kate was there for you *all the time* every day and you were beginning to see her as your mom. He confided in me that he could not have kids and told me that caring for you made Kate happy. And finally, he said he thought I would have a better life if I had a college degree and long-term you would be better off as well. I willingly agreed. It seemed that everyone would win, so we drew up a guardianship agreement and signed off. Legally I would retain parental rights and could see you anytime I wished. If I became self-sufficient, I could terminate the agreement. The agreement included a clause that Kate would be referred to as Mom, and I would be referred to as Aunt Kay. They told me that the rationale was to not confuse you. I found that interesting, because I was the real mom and she was the real aunt."

"But you did become self-sufficient. Didn't you?"

"Yes, I did. After I graduated from law school, I got married to Howard. He took a job here and we bought the house I'm in now. I had to petition the court to get you back. It was not automatic as I had thought. You were eight years old and in a stable, safe environment. The court ruled against me. The argument was that changing the status quo would be traumatic for you. After that, Dan and Kate began the adoption process."

"Did you appeal?"

"I considered it, but my marriage to Howard started going downhill. I didn't pursue it, and in retrospect, I'm glad I didn't. If I had pursued getting you back, it could have put you in harm's way. My marriage to Howard was a mistake. We were married less than three years when I found out his DNA matched that of a fugitive from Kentucky who had raped and killed a minor five years earlier. I divorced him and he went to jail for life."

"My God. I'm sorry. I had no idea. Mom and Dad never mentioned it. I now understand why you want me to know more about Joey before I commit my life to him."

"I hope you don't think I'm being overly protective."

"I don't think that Aunt Kay—or should I now call you Mother?"

"You can call me Mother, but maybe it would be better if you just called me Kay."

"Kay, I want you to know that I'm glad we had this talk and I'm very happy that you are my mother."

"Debra, I'm glad we had this talk as well. I always thought you deserved to know the whole story and it was becoming harder and harder for me to keep it in me. I feel like a heavy load has just been removed."

They had been holding hands for the entire conversation and they had both become misty eyed. They took a moment to recover, and then focused on enjoying their meals. After Kay took the last bite of her salmon, she initiated a new conversation.

"My salmon was very good and I thank you for inviting me here. Have you been here with Joey?"

"Yes, once, and we both liked it."

"Are you planning to go over to his place tonight?"

"Yes, that's okay, isn't it?"

"Yes, of course, but I wanted to talk to you about your relationship. I hope you don't mind, but speaking as your mother now, there are things about your relationship that concern me."

"Like?"

"Now don't get me wrong. I want your relationship to work out. I told you about the mistakes I made. I had a baby before I was ready, and I got married to someone I didn't know very well. Then later I married someone I thought to be perfect and he turned out to be a child rapist. I just don't want you to make the same mistakes I did."

"Yes, I understand. I'm trying to be careful about getting pregnant but sometimes passion overcomes reason. And as far as knowing more about Joey, I have that concern as well. I've heard rumors about who he was before he came to Albuquerque. Like he's not who he says he is; that he's running from the law; that he was an intelligence agent; that he murdered Brandy, and so on."

"Well, I hope you don't mind, but I did a background check on him. Nothing bad showed up, but there are no records of him—absolutely none—prior to 2005 when he came here. So, any one of those conjectures could be true. If you're serious about Joey, maybe it's time to find out. Perhaps you could have a serious talk with him like you just did with me."

"I already tried to have that talk. What he told me was that he worked for the government and what he did was highly classified. At the time, he said he couldn't tell me more than that, but he promised that at some point he will tell me everything. What he said sounded reasonable."

"Do you think his wife knew everything?"

"I asked him that. He said she did, but then he said 'it may have been better if she hadn't.' I wondered why."

"Debra, I hope your life will not be in danger."

"I don't think he would intentionally harm me. I saw how he reacted last weekend and saved that little boy, but maybe he's protecting me."

"I think you need to find out."

"I agree."

Kay looked at her watch. "It's ten o'clock. You don't want him to worry. Maybe you should call him and let him know you're on your way."

After Debra paid the check, she sent Joey a text and gave Kay a very loving goodnight hug.

As she drove towards Joey's house, she felt very relaxed and relieved. She was happy she had that talk with Kay. She couldn't wait to tell Joey about her birth mother. She told him everything that evening.

-35-

CODY CALLS

The next morning, Joey came downstairs leaving Debra to get a few extra snoozes. He stepped out to retrieve the Saturday paper on his front stoop. As he returned the phone was ringing. He raced back to the kitchen, and picked up the receiver, hoping that the extension in the bedroom had not already awakened Debra.

"Hello," he said, a little out of breath.

He heard a familiar recorded message: "Hello, this is Cody. Please enter your code."

Joey knew the call was important. Cody had a high-level position at the U.S. Marshals Service, a bureau within the Department of Justice. The U.S. Marshals Service was responsible for tracking down and arresting federal fugitives. Joey punched in the six-digit code and Cody responded.

"Good morning, Mister Ramirez. I have some updated info for you."

"Something more regarding my wife's death?"

"Yes. We concluded that although it was your car, Brandy was in fact the intended target. We have evidence that the person of interest or POI that we've been looking for planted an explosive device on your car. He followed her from the bar where she met her friends and set it off remotely from his car. The explosion caused the accident. The perpetrator knew that your wife was driving the car and not you. But the accident and explosion didn't kill her."

"How did she die then?"

"The medical examiner in Albuquerque sent a sample of her blood to the FBI lab in Quantico. The FBI found a derivative substance indicating a drug that would have stopped her heart. We now know we're dealing with a secret chemical used by the Russian SVR. We also know we're dealing with a national security issue. The chemical causes death that resembles a heart attack and is virtually undetectable in an autopsy. The CIA has its own version of it. The Albuquerque medical examiner would never have found it. Its existence is highly classified and we can't report what we found back to him."

"Okay, so what about the person of interest. Is he still on the run?"

"We found him. Our POI had returned to Nicaragua. Unfortunately, as a Nicaraguan citizen we couldn't touch him, at least not legally. Unless we can prove his guilt, our treaty with Nicaragua prevents them from extraditing him to the United States."

"Then does that mean you lost the connection between him and the person that hired him?"

"Not at all. We have records of several communications between our POI and Vladimir Petrov. We also have a sighting of the two of them together. And, when the CIA found our POI in Nicaragua, they interrogated him. So, we're quite certain that Petrov of the Russian SVR directed your wife's murder. His motivation is evident. You helped send his comrades in the U.S. to prison. You worked with him while he stole classified information and attempted to kill one of our agents. He trusted you. Then you betrayed him and helped send his comrades to prison. He lost his job and he blames you for that."

"So where is he?"

"It took a while to find him. We talked to your friend Ed Perez. He supported your theory that Petrov was behind this and Perez helped us locate him. Apparently, Perez still has connections. We determined that the SVR removed Petrov from his position as the Costa Rican Chief of Intelligence and sent him back to Russia for reeducation. After that, the SVR allowed him to have a boring desk job at the Russian Consulate in Manhattan. We believe that Petrov blames you for making a fool of him in the eyes of his comrades and superiors and ruining his career. We believe he did this to get back at you."

"I believe that too, but unless we have proof, how can we hold him accountable?"

"Petrov is known to have been in Nicaragua before your wife's murder and there is evidence that he contacted our POI while there. It took a while but we finally traced the message you received after your wife's death back to servers used by the Russian Consulate."

Joey remembered that message.

My love and my career.
Now your turn. See how it feels.

The message had come into his private Gmail account. He had showed it to Ed and later to Cody, but no one else. Then Joey remembered that months later, his boss, Frank, called him into his office and informed him of a message that he had received.

Joey is not who you think he is.
He is fugitive wanted by FBI.

Fortunately, Frank also had a past. It was not by pure chance that he and Frank were working together. They had common contacts in the government and they trusted each other. Joey had told Frank that the message was from the same person that had Brandy killed. "Please keep it to yourself," Joey had told him.

Joey returned his attention to Cody. "Cody, how did Petrov find me?"

"We believe he traced all the people from your past. He visited Alec in prison to learn more about your relationship with Brandy Evans. He traced her and that led to you— probably read about your wedding. That's how he found you. We warned you about that. You broke one of the rules when you reunited with her, but then again, Perez told me you were always a risk taker. You understand that, right?"

Joey took a moment to think about what Cody just said. He was right. As far as the risk was concerned, Joey felt enough guilt without the reminder. But he remembered that he and Brandy both knew the risks when they agreed to get back together, and that helped him deal with it. Then he thought about Ed Perez. If it wasn't for Ed, he would never have been involved with the Russians or met Brandy in the first place. He couldn't blame Ed though. If it wasn't for Ed, he might be dead or in a Costa Rican prison right now. And, he felt grateful that Ed arranged his connection with Cody, rather than with a low-level Deputy Marshal—

"**Ramirez, you still there?**" Cody shouted.

"Yeah, sorry. . . I didn't need your reminder that I may have caused Brandy's death!"

"My apologies," Cody responded.

"So, you're telling me that the Russians know who and where I am. Do you think Petrov is done with me?"

"Take another look at the message he sent after your wife's death. He wanted you to suffer. Killing you would not do that. However, he may try to use what he knows about you to compromise you in some way. However, now that we're onto him, we will track his activity."

"Any chance of arresting him?"

"Not much. He has diplomatic protection, and unless we catch him while committing a crime, nothing we can do—at least not legally.

And, I wouldn't advise the alternative which got us into trouble in the first place."

Assassination, Joey thought.

"What about Alex? When does he get out?"

"Another five years, and as soon as he does, he will be deported back to Russia."

"Well, thanks for the update, Cody. I'll just hang tight for now. But wait, I need to know something before you hang up."

"What?"

"What are the local authorities going to know? I still want to protect my prior identity and I would like that somehow the case can be closed. I don't want it hanging over me."

"The news already speculated that our POI was a "good Samaritan' who heroically saved your wife from the flames. We can support that, but we can also say that he was an illegal immigrant with Nicaraguan citizenship. We can say that he had a wife in the U.S. who was after him for child support. He fled the scene to avoid the publicity and went back to Nicaragua before we could question him."

"That sounds plausible. But what if a private investigator or a curious news correspondent were to go looking for him and he resurfaces?"

"You won't need to worry about that. We've taken care of it," Cody replied.

"Hmmm. I see. But won't the authorities still be looking for a murderer? Isn't there a way to get the case closed before an investigation uncovers the truth?"

"Maybe. It's possible that mechanical failure on the car caused the accident which in turn caused a heart attack. However, given the facts that the authorities already have, that's unlikely. The death investigation team and the medical examiner are dedicated honest professionals. I will ask, but I don't think they will agree to use 'accidental' as the *cause of death* and 'natural' as the *manner of death.* We might convince them to stop investigating due to a national security concern but that could arouse suspicion and you wouldn't want *that* to get into the news. I think a better option is to allow them to keep the cause and manner of death listed as 'undetermined.' Eventually, the case will go cold and everyone will lose interest. They have already cleared you, so you don't need to worry about that."

"Okay, I appreciate you keeping me informed."

They both hung up.

Joey went over to the stove, put on a pot of coffee and started the crossword. He would wait for Debra to come down before preparing breakfast.

Meanwhile, Debra had awakened on the third ring, and she had instinctively picked up the receiver on the stand next to the bed. By the time she got the receiver to her ear, she heard Joey say hello, and someone named Cody say to enter a code. She remembered a phone call weeks earlier when Joey was talking to someone named Cody who he said was keeping him informed of the investigation into his wife's murder.

She could feel her heart beat faster as she depressed the mute button. She knew that listening to Joey's private [phone call was wrong, but her curiosity got the better of her. What she overheard was strange and unsettling. She was hearing about a Joey she didn't know. *Was this the man she wanted to spend her life with?* And yet, what she heard was consistent with what Joey had already told her. She already knew that Brandy had worked for the National Security Agency before moving here and he had told her that he had worked for the U.S. government on highly classified projects. He said he couldn't say too much now, but he promised he would tell her everything when the time was right. The Joey she knew had seemed honest and protective of her, and she had trusted him. After the call ended, she wasn't sure how she felt. She wanted to confront Joey about what she had heard, but she knew she couldn't do that, at least not now. How would he react? She took a few moments to compose herself and then she went into the bathroom to shower.

-36-

FEELINGS

Debra washed and dressed, all the time thinking about that phone call and the advice that Kay had given her the night before. There was no question in her mind that she needed more certainty about Joey and about their future together. She and Joey needed to talk later. She went down to the kitchen and sat at the table. Joey handed her a freshly brewed cup of morning joe, bent down and gave her a kiss.

"Good morning sleepy-head," he said.

"Thank you," she replied with a smile.

"Would you like hot oatmeal topped with fruit yogurt?" he asked. It was her favorite breakfast even in the summer.

"I would, thank you," she replied and then she noticed the crossword he had started. "Wow, a Saturday Times puzzle and you're half done already. I'm impressed." She began reading some of the unanswered clues. Here's an interesting clue—appropriate for breakfast. The clue is 'waffle.' Ten letters in the answer. Can't seem to come up with anything."

"How about *equivocate?*" Joey replied.

"Joey, I don't know what you did for the government, but I think you would have made an excellent intelligence agent." She was baiting him, and took notice that he dropped his serving spoon as she said this.

"You're not so dumb yourself. You may want to consider advancing your career by becoming a medical doctor."

A curious reply she thought, but she gave a serious response.

"Joey, I thought of that, but I think I would rather be a nurse with regular working hours and time for a family life."

"A wise choice. Something I missed out on."

"It's not too late, is it?"

"Don't know. Let's eat."

Joey served the breakfast and they finished the crossword. After breakfast, Debra washed the dishes and cleaned up the kitchen, while Joey tended to the bedroom and bathroom upstairs. When they finished, Joey asked, "What would you like to do today?"

"I assume it will be hot today . . . the pool will be crowded . . . don't know."

"Okay, how about hiking? We can drive up into the mountains where it will be cooler. There's no chance of a storm today, so we should be good. There are many trails up there for hikers. I'll bring a map."

"Sounds good," she replied. "I'll make us sandwiches for lunch."

"I'll pack us four bottles of water," Joey replied. "And my camera," he added.

They got into Joey's Lexus SUV, drove to the east side of the Sandia Mountain Range and onto the scenic Route 536 toward Sandia Crest. Debra enjoyed the scenery of hills, trees, and occasional wildlife. Meanwhile Joey seemed to enjoy negotiating the curves in the winding road as it ascended toward the crest of the mountain range. They finally reached Sandia Crest, parked and walked up to the observation deck and Sandia House, two miles above sea level. They hiked for about five miles or so near the Sandia House. The increased elevation meant that the temperature decreased, making it quite comfortable. They walked to a crest where they could see both Albuquerque to the west and small villages to the east. They took pictures of the spectacular views and pictures of themselves.

It was mid-afternoon by the time they found a picnic area. They sat next to each other as they ate their sandwiches and drank more water. Debra saw this as an opportunity to talk to Joey about their future together.

"Joey, I'm really enjoying this."

"I am also. You know, I really enjoy being with you."

"Joey, I hope I don't spoil the mood with what I'm about to say, but I really need to talk to you about our future."

"What do you mean?"

"Joey, I'm in love with you," she blurted out. "And it scares me."

"Why? We'll work this out, okay?" He looked at her but got no response so he continued.

"Debra I'm in love with you as well. Why are you scared?"

"Because, I don't know what I can expect from you long-term," she said in a soft tone.

"I see. Well, long-term you can expect me to care for you, protect you, and love you."

"And what are you expecting from me long-term?"

"I would like you to marry me and I would like to father a child with you. I've always wanted a child but never had the opportunity."

"Joey, I want the same thing!" she said jubilantly . . . "but I don't think I'm ready."

"I have a concern about that also."

"You do? What is *your* concern?"

"My concern is that it may not be in your best interest right now."

For a moment, she looked surprised by his perceptive and honest assessment.

"Is now the right time? I mean you just started a promising career, and you're still dealing with what your mom did."

She thought about her mom. She had loved her mom, but her mom had manipulated her and taken advantage of her without her even knowing it. And then she went to prison and died. She feared that it could happen again with Joey, especially after overhearing his phone call with Cody. She wanted to trust him but there was much she still didn't know about him.

"You're right. A lot has happened to me over the past year, and I'm still processing some it. I don't think I'm ready to commit to marriage right now. I'm not saying no, I'm just saying I need more time. Okay?"

"I understand. Take as much time as you need. In the meantime, would you consider moving in with me?"

She smiled. "I'll consider it, but I want to talk with Kay first. She just told me she was my birth mother. I don't want her to feel that now I'm going to abandon her."

"It wouldn't have to be all at once. You already live with me on weekends. I just want you to know that you're free to come over anytime day or night. *Mi casa es tu casa*. I don't even need to be there. You already know where the spare key is and you already know the security code, 6342, and . . . you would be closer to where you work."

She giggled and gave him a kiss. "Joey, you don't need to oversell it. We're on the same page. I love you and I want to be in your life. But Joey, there's something else holding me back. I love the part of you that I know. But there is a part of you I know nothing about and I don't know if I will love that part of you and that scares me."

"I see. You know, there are things about you I don't know about."

"Like what?"

"Like the relationships you had with Eddie, your father, and maybe others. But it doesn't matter to me."

She wondered why he would mention the relationship she had with her father, but she let it go.

"But those are all in the past whereas the things I don't know about you are also in the present and may be in the future."

"Look, I know what you're saying, and you will know these things. Just not yet. Believe me, I'm working on it."

"I'm not going to wait forever."

"Understood."

They embraced, packed up their litter, and headed back to the SUV.

***

Back home, later that evening, they were playing pool when he caught Debra staring at her cue stick. She seemed lost in thought.

"Is something troubling you," Joey asked.

"I was just remembering when Dad gave me this stick. He gave it to me when I turned thirteen. It meant something to me."

"You miss him, don't you?"

"I do Joey. I do."

He hugged her, and they went upstairs for the night.

-37-

TEMPTATION

Debra had taken Joey up on his offer. She had moved some of her clothes and toiletries into Joey's house. She stayed at his house on some nights and at Kay's house on other nights. It depended upon her work schedule and which clinic she would report to the next morning. In addition to his new East Side Clinic, Doctor Abraham also had another older clinic, the West Side Clinic. The West Side Clinic was on the northwest side of Albuquerque much further away from Joey's house but closer to Kay's house. Doctor Abraham was very pleased with Debra's work. Patients and staff all liked her. As a registered nurse she became the head nurse at his East Side Clinic. She got a promotion and a salary increase. Her career was everything she could have hoped, and when the head nurse at the West Side Clinic relocated to another state, he asked Debra to cover. So, Debra began working more hours at the West Side clinic and that meant fewer nights at Joey's house. The arrangement was acceptable to everyone and they had no problem adapting.

She and Joey were busy, and they were happy, but their relationship had reached a plateau. Debra needed to spend time advancing her career and needed to know more about Joey's secret life before she would marry him. Joey understood this, but he was afraid to risk her life like he did Brandy's. He hoped the Feds would soon eliminate the threat and the situation would change.

In the meantime, they still found time to socialize and enjoy life. They began socializing more with other people. They had activities with colleagues from her work and with colleagues from his work. They engaged with neighbors, both Joey's and Kay's. They often went to the country club or to dinner, often with other people. They hiked and they played pool. They even tried horseback riding one Sunday. However, they spent fewer nights together and while they were still intimate, the intensity and the passion seemed less than it had been.

Debra began to engage in more activities independent of Joey. She met new friends at work, and had her own activities with them, like after work get togethers, lectures, professional society meetings, and so on. She was pleased that Joey allowed her the independence she needed and did not try to control her. Of course, Joey continued his activities as well, like golf, the firing range, the country club advisory committee and so on. For now, their relationship was satisfactory.

Debra found it easy to make new friends and everyone liked her. One new friend was Ken. Ken worked at the West Side Clinic and that's where they first met. He was a licensed X ray technician. People often came into the West Side Clinic with possible fractures. After Debra examined them, she would often bring them down the hallway to Ken. They had frequently talked at work and had gone out to lunch together once or twice. He was twenty-four years old and good looking. As it turned out the two of them not only shared an interest in medicine, but they also shared an interest in country music. One night in early September she had dinner with Ken. They had worked late that night and it seemed natural to have supper before they headed home—to Kay's house in Debra's case. It seemed innocent enough at first, but then he asked if she would go to a concert with him.

"You mean like a date?" she asked.

"No. Like two friends going to a concert. Two of my other friends will be going as well."

"Who's performing?"

"It's a country group. You told me you liked that kind of music and that you hadn't been to a live concert in a while, so I thought you might like the opportunity."

"When?"

"Next Friday. You'll be working here at the West Side Clinic on Friday, Won't you?"

"Yes."

"So, we can have some supper and go right from here."

She thought she might have some explaining to do if Joey found out, but she needed a change of pace, and it was only a concert, not a marriage proposal.

"Yes," she said. "I'll look forward to it."

She spent Saturday and Sunday nights at Joey's. She told him about the upcoming concert on Friday and that she would be going with friends from work. Of course, she didn't tell Joey who her friend was.

After her shift ended on Friday, she went into the lavatory and changed her whites into appropriate dress for the evening, and added some makeup. When she came out, she was wearing a tan country dress, booty shoes, and her hair in a ponytail. She joined Ken in the lobby. He had also changed out of his work clothes. He was wearing jeans and a western style shirt.

"Wow!" he said. "You really look the part."

"You do as well," she replied.

They went to a local hamburger joint and had a quick supper as planned. Then he suggested that she follow him in her car to his apartment.

"Why?"

"My friends, Mark and Jenny, will meet us at my apartment and we will all drive together in one car. My apartment is closer to the concert, so it will be easier for you as well."

"Sounds reasonable," she said. She followed him to his apartment and parked her car in front of his building.

Mark and his girlfriend Jenny arrived shortly thereafter. After introductions, the four of them got into Ken's car and went to the concert. The concert was not quite what she had hoped for. They had lawn seats but close to the stage—not bad, but it seemed they had more attendees than capacity and the audience was noisy. The performers were supposedly a top-rated country group, but Debra had never heard of them. Smoke, lasers, and special effects augmented their performance, while the music seemed too loud and disjointed. She noted that most of the attendees seemed to be under the age of thirty, like her. There were some teenage girls in the audience that seemed to scream at the start of every new piece. *Was she getting too old for this?* she wondered.

Afterwards, with her ears still ringing, they drove back to Ken's apartment. Apparently, Mark and Jenny were already a couple, judging from their activity in the back seat. When they arrived at Ken's apartment, he insisted that they all come up for a parting nightcap.

"Since you guys are driving," he said to Mark and Debra, "I'm serving coffee and brownies. No alcohol."

Ken served the brownies while Mark served the coffee. Debra took a seat on the sofa and Ken sat next to her. Meanwhile, Mark and Jenny disappeared into the other room. Debra took a sip of her coffee and she and Ken began talking. He made her feel very comfortable and for some reason she didn't mind when he put his arm around her and told her how much he enjoyed being with her. But after a couple more bites of the brownie and a few more sips of her coffee, she started to feel funny. Debra knew something was wrong.

"Ken, what did you put into this coffee?" she asked.

"Nothing, lie back and relax," he said as he moved closer and kissed her gently on the mouth.

"Ken, what are you doing?"

"It's okay, I like you and I think you're very sexy."

Then he was all over her. She felt his hand move up her leg under her dress. As he did this, she began to feel a numbness come over her.

"Ken, please stop. I can't do this with you. Please," she begged. "I'm going to be sick. I need to go to the bathroom." Whether she had lost consciousness or not she wasn't sure, but he eventually stopped. She pulled away and stumbled her way to the bathroom. After locking the door, she relieved herself of the brownies. Feeling dizzy, she sat down on the floor with her back against the wall so as not to fall and hurt herself. She retrieved her phone and called Kay. "I need you to come get me. I'm at . . ." She barely got the address out before she became semi-conscious. While in this state she thought she heard Ken and Mark arguing, and then she heard a door slam.

At some point, she became aware of Ken's voice on the other side of the locked door.

"Debra," he yelled, "Please unlock the door and let me help you. Mark said he laced your coffee with Special K. I didn't mean for this to happen to you. I told him to leave."

"No. Stay away from me."

The next thing she heard was, "Debra, your mother is here! I told her you were not well and shouldn't drive. You need to unlock the door and let her in."

"Debra it's me. It's okay."

Debra could barely move her limbs but managed to make it to the door and let Kay in.

"Debra, what's wrong? Do you need medical attention?"

"No Kay. I'll be okay. Just take me home."

***

Safely home at Kay's house, Debra dozed in an easy-chair where Kay could keep an eye on her. A few hours later she awoke to see Kay right in front of her.

"Are you feeling any better?" Kay asked.

"Yes, I am."

"You want to talk about what happened?"

"Not really. . . I made a mistake. I'm sorry. I really appreciate you coming to get me."

"Please tell me what happened."

"It's embarrassing."

"Embarrassing things happen to the best of us. I'm not one to judge."

"It was just supposed to be a night out with coworkers and friends. We had left our cars at Ken's apartment and when we returned, he asked us in for dessert and coffee. No alcohol, just coffee and dessert . . ."

"And?"

"Well, I sat on the sofa. Ken set a plate of brownies and a cup of coffee on the table in front of me and took a seat next to me. We talked a bit, though I don't remember about what, I took a couple of bites of the brownie and a few sips of the coffee and started to feel funny. I think he put his arm around me and asked if I was okay. I'm not sure how long I was out. The next thing I remember is him trying to have sex with me. That's when I told him to stop. I broke loose, stumbled into the bathroom and locked the door."

"Sounds like he drugged you?"

"That's what I thought. I was feeling sick and don't remember much after that until just before you came. On the other side of the door, I heard Ken and Mark get into an argument and Ken tell Mark and Jenny to leave. Ken said that Mark had laced my coffee with Special K, uh ketamine. The symptoms I had were consistent with that, so I think that's what it was."

"Ketamine is a date rape drug. He tried to rape you. He committed a serious crime. You need to report this."

"I can't!"

"Why?"

"Because we work together. If I reported it, our boss will know and it will affect *my* job as well as his."

"But what if he tries again?"

"I don't think he will—not if he wants to keep his job. He says he didn't know that Mark was going to drug me and I can't prove otherwise ... and although he touched me, he didn't have actual sex with me. And Kay, I don't want Joey to know about this. Please keep it between us."

The next morning, Ken called her cell and apologized, but she wasn't buying it.

"You're lucky I don't charge you with a crime," she said.

"Mark laced the coffee with Ketamine. I didn't know," he insisted. "Debra, we must work together at the clinic. I wish we could have a do-over. I want to make it up to you."

"Ken, I have a regular boyfriend. I can't have that kind of relationship with you. I hope we can keep it professional at work."

"Okay, I hope so," he said and clicked off.

Later, when Joey called, she told him she was not well and would stay at Kay's until Monday. She wasn't sure if she could face him yet. However, her experience with Ken had taught her a lot about herself and about how much she appreciated Joey. Joey trusted her. She vowed never to betray that trust again. She needed him more than ever.

She went back to Joey's place later in the week. When he asked about the concert, she described the performance and said it was not as good as she had expected. Of course, she said nothing about Ken. She and Ken still had to work together and while it remained professional, the tension was high. She felt relieved when Ken left for another job three weeks later.

***

The month of October began with news from Cottonwood, a text message from Susan. Susan had just given birth to a baby boy, Eddie Junior. He came in at a healthy 7 pounds 2 ounces. She posted pictures on social media. Little Eddie was adorable and Debra couldn't help but feel a bit envious. Debra immediately called her to talk.

More good news. She had an offer on the Johnston property in Cornville for $950,000.

"I recommend that you accept it," Susan said. "Don't think you can do any better."

Then Susan provided more detail. "There will be a total commission of five percent for Century, of which I get two and a half," she said. "I've been in touch with your family lawyer. He says there are liens on the house to pay her mom's criminal lawyers and other creditors. Bottom line, you can still expect to net about $825,000."

"Okay, do it," Debra responded. "I trust you."

Debra and Joey continued their 'open' relationship through the month of October. During the second two weeks in October, they attended various events at Albuquerque's annual balloon festival. She went with people from her work; he went with people from his work; and they also went together.

-38-

DISCOVERY

Today was a Monday, the 31st of October, two months after her bad experience with Ken. It was Halloween. Kay expected a large group of kids to show up that evening as they had in the previous year and she was ready. She had lined the kitchen table with boxes of candy the night before. Debra had helped herself to a Riesen candy before bed.

Debra had spent Sunday night at Kay's house because she expected to work at the West Side Clinic in the early part of the week. But when she got up, she didn't feel well. She stumbled into the bathroom. As was the norm, Kay had already left for work because she had a longer drive to work and started earlier. Debra's shift would not start until 9:30. She had time but she was on her own.

Despite feeling nauseous, she forced herself to take her car to the dealership, for what turned out to be a serious engine problem. Appointments were hard to come by and she didn't want to cancel. They had given her a loaner car and she had driven to work afterwards. And, as the day progressed, she had begun to feel better. Perhaps it was just a passing issue she thought, like something she had eaten. Halloween candy?

Then on Tuesday morning, the nausea returned, and it seemed worse. Last night she had helped Kay give out candy to the trick-or-treaters but hadn't eaten any of it. It couldn't be the candy, she reasoned. She made her way to the bathroom, bent over the toilet bowl and unloaded. Then she went to the medicine cabinet. When she came out of the bathroom, several minutes later, she knew exactly what she needed to do. She called in sick to work. She would take the day off and deal with her problem.

Debra drove from Kay's house to Joey's house and took care not to park directly in front of his house. She retrieved the spare key from Joey's hiding place and entered the door. She punched the security code that Joey had given her into the keypad on the wall panel and assured herself that the red light stopped blinking. Then she went to the stairs leading to the lower level and made her way to the file room. She had been in that room once before when Joey had demonstrated his recording device. He never told her the code, and it was months ago. She tried to remember the pattern his fingers made: top left—middle right—top right—bottom center? She wasn't sure of the last one. She punched 1-6-3-8 into the keypad. It didn't work! She took another look at the keys. The number eight key was shiny, but the other keys she had depressed were slightly smudged. The only other key slightly smudged was the number nine key. She tried again. 1-6-3-9. It worked! She opened the door and went in. She tried to remember if there had been a security panel on the wall inside the room. She didn't remember one and she did not see or hear one. All seemed clear, so she began her search.

***

Joey took a bite out of his granola bar and followed with a sip of hot coffee. He had just finished a conference call with a prospective client and was taking a mid-morning break in the few minutes he had before his next meeting. As he set the coffee cup back down on his desk, his smartphone buzzed. It was a security alert indicating a breech to his file room at home. This could be a problem. The file room was where he kept his important legal documents and records, and information he wanted to remain secret. His next meeting was with an important long-time client, but Joey considered the security of his home to be more important. He called his client and explained that he had an emergency at home. He apologized and promised to reschedule.

At this time of day, Joey's company was about twenty minutes away from his home. He drove home and parked the car on the street. Interestingly, he had not received an alert for an unauthorized entry into the home, only an alert for the file room. How could that be, he wondered? As far as he knew, Debra was the only one who had a key and knew the code to turn off the alarm once inside the front or rear doors to the house. Yet, her car was nowhere in sight. He would take no chances. Before exiting the car, he opened the glove compartment, removed his handgun and put it into the side pocket of his jacket. Then he made his way to the front door and entered the main floor of his home as quietly as he could.

Everything on the main floor looked normal. He descended the stairway leading to the lower level, being careful not to step anywhere that creaked. As he made his way through the family room, he noticed that the door to the file room was ajar and the light inside the room was on. He always remembered to turn off the light and close the door when he left. Someone must be in there, he reasoned. He removed the gun from his jacket, and released the safety with his left hand. The gun hung downward from his right arm as he made his way to the door. He slowly pushed the door open, ready to raise the gun. As he did so, he saw Debra sitting on the floor with her back to him. To her right, he noticed a storage box with the lid removed. She seemed engrossed in whatever she was reading. She obviously didn't hear him come in.

"**Debra!**" he shouted.

She jumped to her feet, turned toward him and froze with fear as she noticed the gun.

"Joey, please don't hurt me. I'm sorry," she said excitedly, as Joey continued to move the gun toward the front of his body.

"I would never hurt you," he said as his left hand reset the safety and he returned the gun to his jacket pocket. "I thought you were an intruder. You need to explain yourself. Why are you in here and what are you reading? And by the way, where is your car?"

"My car? It's in for service. I have a loaner. Joey, I know I shouldn't be in here snooping, but I really need to know more about your past. Kay told me she tried to do a background check on you. She says your college has no record of you, and there's no record of your birth. She found no information about you prior to 2005. She also showed me a police report about Brandy's death that suggested you were involved, and apparently, they never actually cleared you. It's still an open case. And, just now, I read a news article from 2004 that says the FBI wanted you for murder and treason. And another article written in Spanish that says you were in a Costa Rican prison. They had your picture but the name was different. Joey . . . who are you?"

"Okay, we need to talk. Let's go into the family room where we can be more comfortable."

She did what he said. After all, he still had the gun.

She took a seat on the sofa and he sat across from her.

-39-

TRUTH

"Debra, I've never hidden the fact that I have a secret past, and I've always promised to tell you everything. I guess this is as good a time as any. I will tell you everything, but it will take a while; it's complicated. I ask you not to make premature judgements. You've seen small bits of a bigger picture and that can be very misleading. I need you to be patient with me until I can tell you the whole story. I also need to warn you that divulging what I'm about to tell you to someone else could put us both in harm's way. Are you okay with that?"

"Okay," she said weakly. She appeared nervous.

"Debra, please relax. I love you. I want you to know that I have never lied to you. Nothing I have ever said to you about myself is untrue. I just haven't told you everything. Let me start by assuring you that I am not a fugitive. I have never killed anyone and I have never been convicted of a crime. However, my life prior to 2005 is a secret. In 2004, I legally changed my name and I entered WITSEC, the federal witness protection program."

"Why WITSEC?" You're not a witness, are you?"

"Yes, I was more than a witness. In 2003 and 2004, I worked with the CIA and the FBI as part of a sting operation. As a result, five Russian spies were charged with attempted murder and espionage. But I was a witness. My secret testimony was crucial in convicting the Russian spies. The Russians are now in prison. So, I'm entitled to protection."

"But why do you still need protection after that?"

"I was a double agent. The Russians thought I was working for them, but later determined that I was a double agent that betrayed them. The phone call that you overheard more than three months ago—and I know you were listening—was from Marshal Cody, my contact in the U.S. Marshals Service. He informed me that they knew with certainty who arranged Brandy's death and how he did it. The so called 'good Samaritan' reported in the news was the one who killed her. The CIA found him in Nicaragua and he talked. He identified the person who arranged her death. His name was Vladimir Petrov. In 2003 he was the head of Russian intelligence in Costa Rica. He was the one that recruited me to work with the Russians."

This was a lot to digest all at once. Debra took a deep breath as Joey continued.

"The Marshals Service tracked Petrov down and found him working at the Russian Consulate in New York City. If he had diplomatic immunity, we couldn't touch him. He remained a potential threat to me and to the people I know. Then last week, Cody informed me that Petrov was missing. He said the marshals could not find him at his residence. He may have learned that his hit man talked and he may have decided to go back to Russia. Or maybe he's holed up inside the consulate. Or he may be dead. Cody said he didn't know."

Debra gave him a look.

"Yeah, I know, but it's best we don't question it."

"Joey, I don't understand. Why would he kill Brandy? Didn't he want to kill *you*?"

"I don't think so. He didn't go to prison but he lost his job because of me. He wanted me to suffer like he did. But he also tried to discredit me and could have blackmailed me to protect my identity."

"What about the others that are in prison. Won't they want to kill you when they get out?"

"Maybe, Alex would. He's the Russian I worked side by side with during the sting operation. Alex was a likable guy and he trusted me. I betrayed him and got him arrested. His mother was a Soviet spy posing as a school teacher in Costa Rica. Someone killed her. Alex and the Russians thought the CIA did it. Specifically, they thought that Brandy's mother did it. But now that Brandy is gone, Alex may be satisfied that I suffered like he did. And besides, he won't be out for another five years, and when he is out, ICE will immediately deport him to Russia. At least that's what we think."

"Did you say they thought Brandy's mother did it?"

"Yes. Brandy's mother was a CIA officer."

"Okay... What about the news article that says you are a fugitive?"

"The news article you found was from a Costa Rican paper. It said I was wanted for murder and espionage. The article was part of my cover, after the sting, so that the Russians wouldn't suspect me of betraying them. At least it worked for a while. But there were others in Costa Rica who may want to either blackmail me or kill me."

"Costa Rica? I don't understand. Did this sting operation take place in Costa Rica?"

Her tone and the look on her face indicated that she may be having difficulty believing what he was telling her was not just a tall tale. But he continued.

"The sting operation began in Costa Rica. I lived and worked in Costa Rica most of my life. I was born in the U.S. as I told you, but my father was Costa Rican. When I was five, he divorced my mom who had become an alcoholic, and we moved to Costa Rica. My father had an advanced degree and had a good job working for the Costa Rican justice department, the OIJ. After I received a graduate degree from Cal Tech as I had told you, I went to work for the Costa Rican Defense Intelligence Service. I wanted to follow in my father's footsteps and clean up corruption in the government, but after three years I became very disillusioned by the bureaucracy I had to work with. I partnered with a guy I had gone to school with and we started a security auditing and consulting company. Business took off, and I felt like I was able to accomplish my career goals."

"So that's why you speak perfect Spanish," she mumbled as his story began to make more sense to her.

"Prior to the sting operation, my client list included several private businesses. My client list also included the CIA. That's when I first met Ed. The Costa Rican government depended heavily on the CIA for international intelligence. So, I had no issue having the CIA as a client. Of course, my work for the CIA was totally secret—"

"Excuse me. Is Ed the same Ed that did the framed photo that hangs over the bed in your bedroom?"

"Yes, one and the same."

"Who *was* Ed?"

"He was the CIA Chief of Station in San Jose. Ed was my contact at the CIA. Interestingly, I first met Ed at the Poás volcano site. That's when he recruited me."

"Okay."

"Another client was a Socialist Party organization. I was not a Socialist, but we shared a common goal to clean up the government. I provided them with intelligence about corrupt officials in the Costa Rican government. Many of them were brought to justice as a result. However, they used my intelligence to advance their cause and get Socialists elected to office. What I didn't know until two years later was that I was working directly for a woman I knew as Maria who had once been a Soviet spy. She had murdered several people in the States, including a CIA officer. The U.S. government had issued a warrant for her arrest and the CIA wanted her to pay for what she did. I also learned that the Socialist Party leaders she worked with were Russian intelligence officers and that Petrov was really her boss and probably her lover as well. Then later, while involved in the sting operation, Alex told me that Maria was his mother."

"So, are you saying that you worked for Russian intelligence and the CIA at the same time . . . and you didn't even know it?"

"Yeah, for a while anyway. I know. I was rather naive, wasn't I? But the CIA used me to their advantage. In early 2003, Petrov requested that I help them by tailing a CIA officer who I knew as Donna. Donna had spent years tracking Russian spies and now she was in San Jose. Petrov feared that Donna would assassinate Maria. With approval from the CIA, I agreed. This is where things got complicated and confusing. As it turned out, someone did assassinate Maria. It was never clear who, but my surveillance supported the idea that the CIA was responsible. Donna was the likely assassin. I personally doubt that was true, but the CIA wanted it to look that way and leaked information to the public to support the idea. The Russians wanted to access Donna's classified files to determine what she knew about their Russian operatives. Then they wanted to assassinate her to make a statement. The CIA used this to their advantage and set a trap for the Russians. The CIA had me offer my services to the Russians to help them accomplish their objective. I was naive enough to believe that after the operation was over, I could resume my normal life in Costa Rica. In retrospect I should've given it more thought. Anyway, I came to the States and hooked up with Brandy to gain access to Donna."

"So, just so I understand this now . . . was Donna Brandy's mother?"

"Yes, one and the same."

"In your files I came across a letter to Brandy from Ed. How did they know each other?"

"Ed and Donna had been close friends and colleagues long before I met them. When Donna died in early March of 2004, Brandy went to Ed and to her birth father Peter for answers. She needed to know why her mother died and she needed to know who I really was."

"The letter indicated that you knew Brandy in 2004. But you told me you met at a conference in Las Vegas in 2010."

"Well, we *re-met* in 2010. I first met Brandy in the States in 2003 at the start of the sting operation."

"Was she part of the operation?"

"No, Brandy knew nothing of the operation until after her mother died."

"Joey, I'm getting confused again. Donna died. Did you help the Russians kill her?"

"No of course not. We . . . the CIA that is . . . couldn't let that happen, and part of my job was to assure that it didn't. But we wanted the Russians to believe they had killed her. Donna died of the cancer she already had, but she had kept her cancer a secret. The Russians thought it was their poison that killed her."

"And what did Brandy think?"

"Like I said, she didn't know how her mother died until later. She didn't know anything about my mission either. She thought I was in the States on business working with one of my business clients to design and implement a new security system. It was necessary for me to get to know her as part of the role I was playing with the Russians. We dated, but after her mom died, she thought the worst of me—thought that I may have killed her. After I was in custody, Ed and Brandy's birth father, Peter, helped her to understand what really happened and who I really was. They arranged for me to have a meeting with her before I went into WITSEC. I apologized profusely and to this day I feel badly about how I misled her. Her parting words in 2004 were that she hoped that someday she could forgive me and we could find each other and start over again. I wished the same thing but never thought it could realistically happen—that is until 2010 in Las Vegas."

"You're lucky she took you back. I'm not sure you deserved it."

"You're right, I probably didn't, but even after six years we still loved each other. Our dream to start over came true, except that as fate would have it, it cost her life."

"Are you still working for the CIA or the FBI?" I need to know."

"No. Never again! My involvement with them pretty much ruined my life."

"What about Brandy's car accident? The newspapers said that it was suspicious and under investigation. They suggested that you might have had something to do with it."

"It *was* suspicious, especially to me it was. But what people don't know is that I initiated the investigation by the Feds. I received a message after Brandy died that I thought may have come from came from Petrov, suggesting that he may have ordered her murder. Only I wasn't sure. I gave the message to the Feds and ultimately, they determined its source. But, no one can know that, including the local authorities!"

"But doesn't that mean that it's still an open case? Won't the State Police and the local authorities eventually find out the truth?"

"Yes, it is an open case, but the local investigators will never solve it. According to Cody, the public will never know the identity of the actual killer—the so-called good Samaritan. The information is classified. And without that, an investigation will not learn about Petrov or about my background. I could have been the killer, but I was out of town. The local investigators did consider the possibility that someone tampered with the car, but it was my car and I drove it before I left. It could have been an accident, but there's no way Brandy could have lost control. She drove my Audi many times. She drove that road many times, even in bad weather, and a toxicology found no drugs or excessive alcohol in Brandy's system—Debra, you look like you want to say something."

"Joey, you've given me a lot to think about. My head is spinning with information overload right now. I wish we had this conversation earlier in our relationship."

"Well, perhaps we should have, and I know this is a lot all at once. But only hearing part of it, may have led you to false conclusions. Also, I didn't want to scare you, and I wanted to be sure that you would keep what I told you between us. Any leaks to other people, intentional or unintentional, could result in harm to both of us. I didn't want to see you murdered like Brandy. And to be honest, I was afraid of how you would react. And even now I'm afraid that after hearing all this, you might decide that you don't love me enough to want to be with me anymore. I'm sorry, I need to take a break and get some air."

She could hear the emotion in his voice as he said this. Joey stood up and walked outside to the lower deck.

Debra could hear the emotion in his voice as he said this. She watched him stand up and walk outside to the lower deck. She paused to reflect for a few moments. Joey certainly had a whopper of a life story. If someone had revealed his story to her all at once before she knew him, she may not have believed it. But all the pieces fit and she had no reason to question it. Joey had given her reason to believe in him as well. He was honest with her, compassionate toward others, and he treated her well. She knew that what she did and said next would change both their lives. Yet she was more sure of her decision now than ever. She followed Joey out onto the deck.

***

Joey was standing on the outer edge of the deck staring at the distant mountains. Debbie walked up behind him and put her arms around him in a bear hug.

"Joey, please don't be upset with me. I still love you, and I still want to be with you," she said with conviction. "You've been nothing but good and supportive of me since the day I met you. And you've been honest with me. But Joey, now it's my turn to be open and honest with you."

He turned around to face her. "What do you mean?"

"I needed to find out about your past as soon as possible because I had a decision to make." He looked at her quizzically.

"I found out this morning that I'm pregnant," she stated with trepidation.

"Oh . . . that's good . . . isn't it?"

"I don't know, Joey. I thought we were being careful."

"I thought so too. Perhaps it was that night we fell asleep while I was still in you and the condom came off."

She remembered how they had laughed about it at the time. "Yes, I remember," she chuckled.

"How far along are you?"

"Probably two months."

"Hmm . . . Are you sure I'm the father?"

She could tell from his tone that he was serious. "Joey, why would you ask me that?"

"Because two months ago you were with Ken."

There was a moment of stone silence before she responded.

"Ken? How did you know about Ken? Did Kay tell you? I think Ken drugged me. I called Kay to come and rescue me. I asked her not to let you know."

"Kay didn't tell me, but I was hoping you would. Let's just say I pieced it together from several sources including you and including your boss."

"Joey, Ken was a mistake and we never had intercourse. Please forgive me for that!"

"It's okay, I already have. Look, I understood your need to test and understand your feelings. I also respect your independence. I will never try to control you and tell you what you must do. But more importantly, I'm glad to know that you didn't have intercourse with him. That would have complicated things for us." He paused for a moment. "Debra, tell me what *you* want to do. Were you considering an abortion?"

"Well, before our conversation, I considered all my options. I feared the worst about you and I wasn't sure I should tell you, or how you would react. But now, I want you to be part of the decision. Tell me what *you* want."

"Debra, I love you and I want to raise this child with you, and I believe we can do it together, but only if it's what *you* want."

A smile spread across her face. "It *is* what I want," she answered.

"Then, Debra, there's something I want to ask you."

"What's that?"

"Will you marry me?"

Her face lit up and her eyes swelled with tears of joy as she kissed him hard on the mouth.

"YES, YES, YES"!

-40-

MOVING ON

With the help of Kay, Debra and Joey planned their wedding. Timing was important. It would be before Debra looked pregnant, yet with enough time for people to plan. It also needed to be at least six weeks after Susan's baby was born. Debra wanted Susan to be her Matron of Honor. They decided to have a December wedding after Christmas and before the new year. Joey made arrangements with his country club. Kay arranged for a neutral minister. She would walk Debra down the aisle, and Joey's business partner would be his best man. They invited 75 people to include all their friends and colleagues from work and from their local neighborhoods. They also invited out-of-town friends and family, like friends from Cottonwood. It was only two months away so they would offer free lodging to those who needed it. And although unlikely to come, they also invited Brandy's birth father Peter and wife, Brandy's son Brian and wife, and Joey's family friend Ed.

***

Ed Perez sat in front of his desktop computer at his home on the outskirts of San Jose, Costa Rica. He was thinking about his reply to Joey's wedding invitation and note. Joey and Debra were getting married and Joey had let slip that they had a child on the way. The wedding would be on the last Saturday in December at Joey's country club. They expected up to 50 people to attend. *Interesting,* Ed thought. He had never met Debra. *I'd really like to meet Debra. Wish I could go,* he thought to himself, *but Joey said he would understand if I declined.*

Ed reflected on his relationship with Joey. Ed was thirty years older than Joey but Joey reminded him of his earlier years. Ed always liked him. He knew Joey Ramirez as Joe Garcia Martinez. Joe worked undercover. He kept Ed informed of Socialist activities and Russian influence in Costa Rica. Ed had encouraged Joe to participate in the sting operation, and he felt partly responsible for the harmful aftermath. He felt he owed it to Joe to provide all the support for him that he could.

Joe became involved with Brandy during the sting operation. After the sting operation, in 2004, Joe had taken refuge at the U.S. Embassy in Costa Rica. Ed had visited Joe every day during the ten weeks he was there. During this time, Ed got to know him on a personal basis. He helped Joe get a fair deal with the CIA and the FBI, and he helped to arrange for Joe to apologize and say goodbye to Brandy. Shortly thereafter, Joe disappeared into WITSEC.

Ed also knew Brandy's mom, Donna. Over the years, they had worked on several intelligence operations together. Eventually, they had been intimate and Ed hoped that they would retire together in Costa Rica. Unfortunately, the return of Donna's cancer scuttled that idea. But they remained close. Donna knew the Russians planned to kill her and she feared that they might harm Brandy as well. Before Donna died, Ed promised to give Brandy the protection she needed.

After Donna's death and Joey's disappearance, Ed had kept in touch with Brandy. But when he visited Brandy in the States in 2011, he was surprised to learn that she had reunited with Joe—now Joey Ramirez—and would marry him. He warned them of the risk, but to no avail. Out of concern for Joey and Brandy's safety, he didn't go to their wedding, but he sent them one of his prize photos as a wedding gift. Although he kept in touch by mail, he didn't see Joey again until Brandy's funeral in 2015. Now he felt that he had let Donna down. He hadn't protected Brandy and he had caused Joey to suffer even more. He owed them both. He vowed to do everything he could to bring their enemy to justice. And he had done just that.

Before clicking 'send' Ed reviewed his response to Joey's invitation.

Joey,

I very much appreciate your invitation but will not attend. You said that you would understand. Of course, I wish you the best. I am pleased that you are moving on with your life, and that you found someone who will restore the meaning and joy you deserve. Fatherhood is something I never had, so for that I envy you.

You asked how I was doing. All things considered (old age) I'm doing quite well. I keep busy with my photography. I've attached a current picture of the Poás volcano. As you can see, it looks different than it did in 2002. There have been several eruptions. Not a place you want to be now.

Last year we talked about climate change. Thanks to the Chinese, the solar power industry is starting to takeoff, and there are major improvements to our highway system. In 2003 we were so concerned about the Russians taking over through political influence. But it seems that now the Chinese are taking over through economic influence. In any case, the country is more socialistic now. By the way, your socialist friend Judi is now a member of the Assembly. She thinks you're dead or in prison as do many others here. Don't risk coming back.

Oh, by the way, I'm expecting Peter and Carol to visit in February. We haven't seen each other since Brandy passed. It's a tour group, and they will come early for a short visit beforehand. I was hoping Brian and his wife might come as well but it seems only old people go on these tours.

PETER EISENHUT

Speaking of which, I'm getting old myself and my health isn't getting any better. Don't know how long I will be around. When I go, Peter Troutman will get the notice and he'll let the rest of you know. Oh, I don't know if Brandy told you about the fund that I had set up with her mom Donna many years ago. When Donna died, I became the sole owner and made Brandy the beneficiary, but now that she's gone, I've made you and Brian the beneficiaries. Brian already received some of the money for his education, but I have not needed any of it for my living expenses so there will be plenty left.

I often think back on my life and I know you have thought back on yours as well. We questioned if things could have been different had we done this or that. We recently talked about it. I know you felt some guilt with respect to Brandy's death. But it does no good to ask 'what if?' after the fact. We could never know the answer. We did the best we could with what we knew at the time. Our fate is difficult to predict.

I still spend much of my time keeping up with current international news, an interest I've always had. Last week, I came across a news article I thought might interest you. Utility workers found the dead body of a man only three blocks away from the Russian Consulate in New York. He had no identification on him but my sources say that the body belongs to Vladimir Petrov. It's a shame how crime is taking over the cities in the U.S. isn't it?

I'm pleased that you are moving on with your life. I wish you and Debra a good and safe life together, and I really mean that.

Your friend,
Ed

Enclosed article:
UTILITY WORKERS DISCOVERED A BODY INSIDE A MANHOLE ON TUESDAY MORNING. THE STARTLING DISCOVERY WAS MADE AROUND 3 A.M. TUESDAY MORNING IN THE AREA BETWEEN 5TH

AVE. AND EAST DRIVE NEAR 91ST STREET ON THE UPPER EAST SIDE OF MANHATTAN. UPON ARRIVAL, POLICE OFFICERS OBSERVED THE DECOMPOSED BODY OF AN UNIDENTIFIED ADULT MALE. IT'S NOT IMMEDIATELY CLEAR HOW LONG THE BODY WAS INSIDE THE MANHOLE BEFORE IT WAS FOUND. THE BODY IS NOW BEING CHECKED BY A MEDICAL EXAMINER TO DETERMINE CAUSE OF DEATH AND HELP IDENTIFY THE PERSON.

POLICE SAY THE INVESTIGATION OF THE INCIDENT IS ONGOING.

Jane Clark, Reporter, The Daily News

Ed clicked the 'send' key. Then he reached for something on the back of his desk. He held it in his hand and smiled. It was a photo ID for the Russian Consulate. The name under the photo was Vladimir Petrov.

***

When Joey received Ed's reply, he showed it to Debra. "I think he's given you a clear message that it's not safe for you to go back to Costa Rica," she said.

"Yeah. As much as I miss my years there, it's probably not worth the risk."

"Joey, he said a couple of things I don't understand. "What was that fund that he mentioned?"

"I don't know much about it—only what Brandy had mentioned. Apparently, when Ed was in the field with Donna, they put their per diem money into an investment fund. By the time Brandy died it was worth millions. Some of it went toward Brian's education, but that's about all I know."

"Per diem? Millions? Does that sound legit?"

"Never really thought about it."

"And Joey, there's something else I don't understand. Cody told you that Petrov was missing, didn't he? But Ed's telling you that he's dead."

"Interesting, isn't it?"

ACKNOWLEDGEMENTS

I would like to start by thanking my wife Jean for understanding my need to write and for the effort she put into reviewing all my drafts. I also want to thank my friend Bob Greiner for the effort he put into doing a thorough job of copy editing.

    I also thank my beta readers. They reviewed my pre-published manuscripts and provided valuable feedback. I thank my colleague and friend Byron Battles and my friend Ellen Sosinski for their honest and constructive reviews. I also thank my long-term friend George Fleischman for his positive comments and for his encouragement.

ABOUT THE AUTHOR

Peter S. Eisenhut is a graduate of Cornell University and the University of Rochester. He worked for two international organizations and as an independent consultant. He now spends his time doing volunteer work, hiking, and writing. The inspiration for his novels comes from his career experiences and his travels. *Fateful Affairs* follows his third novel, *Final Project*, his second novel, *The Boulder Creek Project* and his first novel, *The Pen Project*.

Peter lives in Columbia Maryland with his wife Jean. For more information, visit Peter's author page on Amazon at: https://amazon.com/author/petereisenhut-usa.
Or, his website at https://www.petereisenhut-author.com .

CPSIA information can be obtained
at www.ICGtesting.com
Printed in the USA
LVHW031708090723
751946LV00003B/420